Garth Jennings has directed many music videos and commercials. His work includes videos for Blur, Radiohead, Beck, Fatboy Slim and Vampire Weekend.

He is the director of three feature films: *The Hitchhiker's Guide to the Galaxy* (2005); *Son of Rambow* (2007), for which he also wrote the screenplay; and Golden Globe-nominated *Sing* (2016), a feature-length animated film with an all-star cast, from the studio that created *Despicable Me*. He has also written *The Wildest Cowboy*, a picture book, for Macmillan Children's Books.

THE GOOD, THE BAD AND THE DEADLY

GARTH JENNINGS

MACMILLAN CHILDREN'S BOOKS

Published in 2019 by Macmillan Children's Books
an imprint of Pan Macmillan
20 New Wharf Road, London N1 9RR
Associated companies throughout the world
www.panmacmillan.com

ISBN 978-1-5098-8765-1

1 3 5 7 9 8 6 4 2

A CIP catalogue record for this book is available from
the British Library.

Printed and bound by CPI Group (UK) Ltd, Croydon CR0 4YY

For Leo

LOOK AT THE PIGLET

You're just in time.

I'm afraid life is about to take a terrible turn for twelve-year-old Nelson Green. Well, the good times had to come to an end sooner or later, didn't they? Having spent a glorious summer goofing around North East London with seven knee-high monsters invisible to everyone but him, Nelson and his monster friends are now being separated by forces beyond their control. And, as if that weren't enough, they are about to face a creature who threatens to end all life on earth by Monday morning at the latest. I strongly suggest you take a good, long look at this drawing of a piglet in pyjamas, as it will be the last time you see or read about anything nice for a while.

Having enjoyed the piglet, I hope you are now feeling prepared to plunge back into the story, but before I can reveal what has become of Nelson and his monsters, I must take you back to the time this story truly began. And like so many incredible stories, this one begins in the dark.

THIS WICKED BUSINESS

LONDON. 1667. WAY PAST BEDTIME . . .

'Father . . . Father, wake up . . . Wake up,' whispered Jane, but Sir Christopher Wren (the world-famous architect, mathematician, scientist, astronomer, inventor, and wearer of huge curly wigs) continued to snore like a donkey. It was the fifth night in a row that he had fallen asleep at his desk while trying to redesign the handrail for the Whispering Gallery of St Paul's Cathedral. Not that you could see his designs in the smoke-flavoured darkness of his study, or anything else for that matter. The candles had burned out hours ago, and the fire that had been keeping him warm was nothing but rustling ash now. The

only light came from the little candle that Jane was holding in front of her.

'Father . . . Father . . . Wake up,' Jane whispered again, but it wasn't until she gently prodded the end of his long nose that the snoring stopped and his eyes fluttered open.

'Ahh . . . hello, Jane,' mumbled Sir Christopher, and he smiled at the sight of his daughter's heart-shaped face in the candlelight.

'Should I let him in, Father?' asked Jane.

'Let who in, my darling?'

'The man.'

'What man?'

Jane replied by pointing to the window behind her father where a ghostly pale face was staring at them both through the glass.

'Waah!' yelped Sir Christopher as he jumped out of his chair, sending his paperwork scattering all over the place and his telescope crashing to the floor.

Jane raised her candle to the window for a better look at the fellow.

Underneath a hood made of sackcloth, Jane's candle illuminated a hairless and wrinkled man's face decorated with two baggy, bloodshot eyes and a nose that had been squashed flat in his youth by a kick from a startled horse.

It might sound creepy to you, but this squashy face actually belonged to a good soul, and the goodness shone through his smile.

Sir Christopher let out a loud sigh of relief and gently moved Jane to one side in order to open the window. 'Nothing to be frightened of, Jane. It is just my horseman, Bailey,' said Sir Christopher, although it was clear Jane wasn't in the least bit frightened.

'Bailey. It's the middle of the night.'

'Forgive me, my lord,' said Bailey, who sounded like a breathless toad. 'But there is proper trouble brewin' up at St Paul's.'

'Oh, not the stone thieves *again*,' groaned Sir Christopher while resetting his telescope on its tripod.

'No, my lord. Not thieves. 'Tis Master Buzzard.'

'Master Buzzard? Oh, what has that overfed buffoon done now?'

''Tis not what Master Buzzard has done, my lord,' said Bailey pulling himself up so that his face was leaning in through the open window. 'Tis what he is a-plannin' to do with . . . with the *extractor*.'

'The *extractor*?'

'Yes, my lord. The extractor.'

'Well, he's wasting his time with the extractor – it doesn't work.'

'But, my lord, I fear Master Buzzard may have found a way to *make it work*.' Bailey bowed his head a little as if this were very grave news, and judging by the stunned look on Sir Christopher's face, it was.

'What's an extractor?' interrupted Jane eagerly, but Sir Christopher did not look keen to answer her.

'Uh . . . just a device I . . . I should have never bothered with.'

'Why? What does it do?'

'What does it do? Oh . . . well, one day I will answer that question, but right now I must go to the cathedral and make sure that colossal dunderhead Master Buzzard doesn't do anything with it.' Sir Christopher bent over to fasten the buckles on his chunky high-heeled shoes, which, along with extremely big wigs, were the height of men's fashion at that time.

'Dunderhead' was just one of the many words Jane had heard her father use when describing his apprentice, Master Buzzard. She had also heard her father use words like 'buffoon' and 'dimwit' and 'nincompoop' quite a lot too, and it was clear that if Master Buzzard had not been the son of a very powerful and wealthy duke, there was no way he would still be her father's apprentice.

'I shall fetch our coats, Father,' said Jane, as if they had just been invited to an exciting party.

'Coats? No, no, no. Jane, you are to stay here and go back to bed.'

'But I could help you.'

'Jane, you will have no part in this wicked business—'

'Please!'

'It's too dangerous,' snapped Sir Christopher.

'Then why are you going?'

'Because . . . Please . . . just . . . just go back to bed. And in the morning we'll have more of that lovely raspberry jam we made together. I shall collect fresh bread on my way home. I promise.' Sir Christopher kissed the top of her head before adjusting his enormous wig in the mirror and rushing out into the hallway where he knocked over several walking sticks and a pot that had been catching rain from a leak in the roof.

'*Raspberry jam?* I don't care about raspberry jam – I want to come with you!' she called out, but it was too late. Jane could hear her father's silly shoes clattering across the courtyard and his grunts of effort as he struggled to open the rusty bolt on the back gate. She turned to look out of the window and saw Bailey climbing into the front seat of a stagecoach ready to be pulled by two eager white horses. Jane reached out as if to close the window, but

she didn't. She didn't turn to go back up to bed either. Instead, she opened the window wider, blew out her candle and vanished into the darkness.

The stagecoach hurtled through the narrow streets of London. There was so much clattering and shouting and

thundering of hooves that neither Sir Christopher Wren nor his driver Bailey heard Jane giggling below inside the carriage.

How did Jane get inside the carriage? Well, in those few chaotic seconds while her father had been wrestling with the back gate, Jane had climbed out of her father's study window and snuck aboard. There was no way someone as curious as Jane could have gone to bed without finding out what this thing called an 'extractor' was capable of doing, and – even more intriguing – why the 'dunderhead' called Master Buzzard would go to such lengths to test it in the middle of the night.

THE ABOMINATIONS OF MASTER BUZZARD

Jane hid inside the carriage until the stagecoach had stopped moving and she was sure her father and his driver Bailey were some distance away. When at last she dared to peep out of the window, Jane could clearly see the moonlit silhouette of what was to be her father's most famous contribution to London's skyline: St Paul's Cathedral. It was a breathtaking sight despite being far from finished and surrounded by all the muck and mess you would expect to find on such a vast building site.

Silk slippers were not made for scrambling over great piles of rock and stone, but Jane was too concerned with finding out what was going on

inside the cathedral to care. Gusts of icy wind rushed up from the River Thames and whirled around Jane as if to say, 'Turn around, Jane! Go back! Go back!' But the wind was wasting its breath.

Meanwhile, Sir Christopher and Bailey had reached the top of the stairs to the first floor of the cathedral, each carrying an oil lamp. Though both of them panted like dogs, they didn't stop running until they had burst through the door of the laboratory to find the man responsible for tonight's hoo-ha. (I know that many of you will not be familiar with the term 'hoo-ha' because it is a very old-fashioned way of describing a big fuss. However, I like 'hoo-ha', and I'm determined to bring it back into everyday use along with some other classics like 'shiver me timbers' and 'I should coco'.)

BANG! went the door as it hit the wall.

'Master Buzzard! What in the name of Sweet Hosanna do you think you are doing?!' blurted Sir Christopher between great gulps of air.

A man who looked like an oversized chubby baby, dressed in the fanciest clothes money could buy, turned to look at him with surprise on his powdered white face. This was William James Henry William Layton Buzzard (yes, his parents actually named him William twice). He was the dimwit, the numbskull, the overfed buffoon that had been such a troublesome apprentice to Sir Christopher.

William James Henry William Layton Buzzard

You certainly won't recognize the two hooded thugs he had paid to protect him, or the artist he had paid to paint his portrait, but some of you might recognize the table they are all standing next to. This is the sin extractor.

The two thugs rushed across the

room and pinned Bailey and Sir Christopher to the wall.

'Let go of us at once!' barked Sir Christopher. 'This is my office! You have no right to be here!'

'Hush now, hush now,' said Master Buzzard, touching the tip of his finger to his puffy top lip. 'Can't you see? I am having my portrait painted and I cannot move from this elegant pose until Robert has captured me at my best and most heroic.'

Robert the painter was as thin and shrivelled as a waterlogged finger and wore an equally wrinkly leather apron. On his canvas, Sir Christopher could see the beginnings of a flattering portrait, including the sin extractor.

'This is neither the time nor the place to have your ghastly image painted. Now get out!' Sir Christopher's rage made everyone in the room, including the thugs, jump.

'I have more than enough to be going with, Master Buzzard,' muttered Robert the painter, and with one swift movement, he grabbed the easel, portrait and brushes and headed for the door.

Buzzard called out after him. 'Oh very good, Robert. And don't forget – you are not only capturing my noble appearance, but also the moment I, William Buzzard, made history.'

'You? Make history? HA! You know very well I have tested this device twenty times, even on Bailey, and it did nothing more than give him a nasty rash,' said Sir Christopher.

Bailey nodded emphatically. 'It did, my lord! A terrible rash it was too. All over me backside. I was scratching me bottom day and night.'

'Well, I am the reason it never worked,' said Buzzard proudly. 'Because I had always disconnected it here.' Buzzard crouched and pointed to the copper wires dangling beneath the table.

'You see, sir,' said Master Buzzard with a grin, 'I am not just a pretty face.'

'How dare you meddle with my work!' hissed Sir Christopher through gritted teeth, but this only made the thugs tighten their grip on him.

'Well, one must be creative if one wants to make a name for oneself.'

'Oh, it's a name "one" wants, is it? Well I have plenty of names for you!'

Master Buzzard's babyish demeanour was replaced by a horrid little snarl that made his right nostril flare wide enough to fit a grape inside it. (Please don't try fitting a grape up your nose. It will end in tears.)

'Yes . . . I have heard the names you call me behind my back. What? You think I didn't hear you? Well, I believe some of those names may suit *you* now, sir!'

Buzzard took off his shoes to reveal stockinged feet.

'When his Majesty King George learns what I have done tonight – that it was I, William Buzzard, who created a machine that can cleanse even the most wicked souls of evil – he will reward me with riches beyond my wildest dreams. My portrait shall hang beside the great and the good. I shall be famous throughout the empire. Throughout time! Now, please remain silent while I carry out the extraction, or I will have my men break both your noses.'

Sir Christopher felt the thug tighten his grip and decided to do as he was told. The extractor creaked as Master Buzzard heaved his great buttocks on to the edge of the table, then he closed his eyes and gently rolled his body backwards. Buzzard gasped, wide-eyed with surprise as the thousands of tiny silver needles pierced the skin on his back. You would have expected him to scream, but instead he appeared to slowly relax as if he were settling on to a soft mattress.

There was a loud *hisssssss* like a punctured bicycle tyre, and the extractor table began to vibrate. Beneath the table, the seven copper test tubes rattled. Whatever was being extracted from Master Buzzard was being collected in these seven tubes, steam rising from each one until they were all whistling like eager little trains.

I order you to stop this at once! is what Sir Christopher should have said, but his curiosity, that great fizzing part of his brain that wanted to understand and unravel all the mysteries of the universe, smothered his common sense in a blanket of questions. Was his vain and stupid apprentice really about to make his sin extractor work? Could the human soul be cleansed of all wickedness? Is it really possible to separate the good from the bad in a human being?

The hissing and rattling noises made by the sin extractor were gradually accompanied by another sound. It was a deep rumbling, like distant thunder, coming from somewhere else in the cathedral. None of the men in the laboratory had any idea what was making this sound, but Jane did.

She was crouched behind the door to her father's laboratory and had been peering through the keyhole when hundreds and hundreds of rats emerged from the walls and under the doors until the floor was just a river

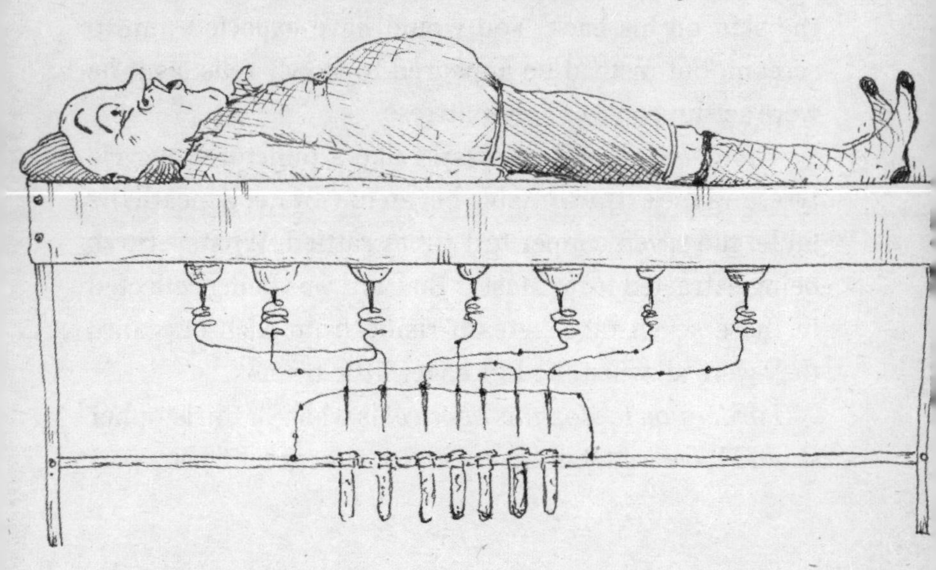

of oily black fur. As you know, Jane is not the kind to be easily frightened – but *rats*? Jane loathed rats, which is why she leaped on top of a wooden crate. She needn't have worried though. None of those rats were interested in Jane. They were only concerned with getting out of St Paul's and away from the extractor as quickly as possible. And you are about to find out why.

Master Buzzard sprang up into the air as if the sin extractor had suddenly been charged with electricity.

'Aaaargh!' he screamed, and he staggered across the room before crumpling to the floor. At the very same time, the seven copper vials beneath the table toppled to the floor.

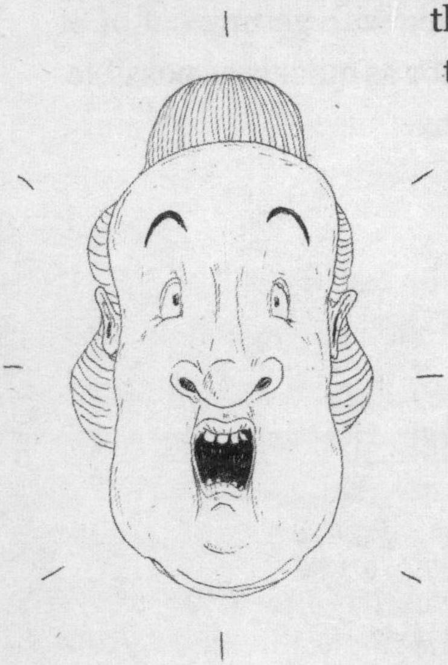

Outside the laboratory door, as rats scattered away across the floor, Jane jumped down from the crate to peer back through the keyhole.

Master Buzzard appeared to be as delighted as he was breathless.

'Oh my! For a moment there, I felt such bliss. Pure, golden bliss. I had a memory from my youth. No, it was more than just a memory. I was really there. Yes, I sat upon my mother's knee as she fed me cake and told me what a beautiful boy I was and that I would grow up to be famous,' he said breathlessly, although no one else in the room could see anything but Buzzard grinning like a fool.

'He's gone off his rocker, my lord,' whispered Bailey.

'He was never on his rocker in the first place,' said Sir Christopher.

'What's this? Monsters?' whispered Master Buzzard. The happiness he had been feeling had vanished and he now wore the expression of a giant frightened baby.

'Oh, for heaven's sake. There are no cakes and there are no monsters. Guards! Thugs! Whatever you are! Get this ignoramus back to his home before he starts to see dancing fairies or singing sprites,' commanded Sir Christopher, and the hooded guards nodded eagerly in agreement. They may have been thugs, but they were smart enough to know when to switch to the winning team.

'Monsters!' screamed Master Buzzard.

Jane found his cry so chilling that her stomach seemed to shrink to the size of a walnut.

'Look! On the floor! There! Argh! Get them away from me! Please! Get them away from me,' panted Buzzard. He grabbed the nearest thing to him, which was a bucket of ash beside the fire, and hurled it towards the middle of the room. It clattered on the stone floor and filled the air with a cloud of ash.

'The devil has sent his monsters for me!' wailed Buzzard as he scrambled for the door, threw it open and ran for his life.

'Stop all this nonsense and get back here at once!' said Sir Christopher as he coughed and swatted at the ash floating in the air around him.

'What have I done?' cried Buzzard as he ran down the corridor, and he would have cried other things too had he not tripped over the rats that swarmed under his feet.

'No! Stop! Don't go any further!' cried Sir Christopher.

But it was too late. Buzzard had tumbled towards a balcony overlooking the great hall of the cathedral. It wouldn't have been so bad had there been a handrail, but it hadn't been built yet. The scream Buzzard made as he fell to the floor of St Paul's was not nearly as chilling as the sudden silence as he hit the ground.

Jane crouched by the door feeling very cold and frightened. She would have run as fast as she could back to the carriage had she not heard the sound of boots approaching on the other side of the door. Jane watched as the hooded thugs rushed out of the laboratory followed by Sir Christopher and Bailey.

'Stop! There's no chance Buzzard could have survived that fall,' said her father with barely stifled anger. 'Take his body back to his home and tell anyone who asks that he died in a drunken brawl at a tavern. And mark my words – unless you want to lose your heads, I suggest you both take what you have seen here tonight to your graves.'

The thugs seemed to swallow Sir Christopher's words as if they were a mouthful of nasty medicine before running away.

'Father – look!' cried Jane, and Sir Christopher nearly jumped out of his silly shoes. You might have thought Jane was crazy to draw attention to herself now, but she had a very good reason to call out to him.

'*Jane?* What in the name of pickles and pears are you doing here?'

'I know I shouldn't have come, and I'm sorry. But,

Father – look. There! On the floor!'

The cloud of ash had settled, revealing something that until now had been invisible to everyone but Master Buzzard: bizarre little creatures were moving on the stone laboratory floor. There were seven of them, each one about the size of a large fruit or vegetable. One looked like a tongue wriggling and licking the air. Another was a gelatinous ball rolling around as it swelled in size. Another appeared to be a tentacle that snaked its way across the floor.

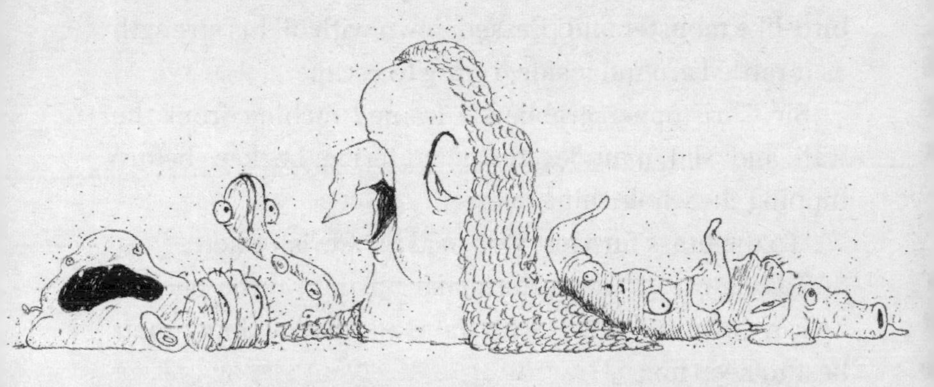

'Master Buzzard's sins,' wheezed Bailey as he made the sign of the cross on his chest.

Bailey was right. That's exactly what they were. Seven sins brought into existence as living organisms, but one in particular was much bigger than all the others. It was a bird-like creature with a very large beak and, by the looks of it, an equally large appetite. No sooner had it taken form than it lunged towards the wriggling tentacle, gobbling it up as if it were a giant worm.

'Stay back!' said Sir Christopher.

The ash-covered bird monster clearly didn't feel the tentacle was a satisfying enough meal as it then began scoffing the remaining creatures. Chomp! Chomp! Chomp! Within just a few seconds, it had swollen to the size of a plump chicken, and when it realized there was nothing more on the floor left to eat, it looked around hungrily and turned towards Jane.

BLAM! Bailey slammed the empty ash bucket over the bird-like monster and pressed down with all his strength as it rattled around inside, trying to escape.

Sir Christopher grabbed a framed etching from the wall and slid it under the shuddering bucket, before flipping the whole thing over.

'To the brass furnace! Go!' said Sir Christopher.

Taking care to keep the makeshift lid on the bucket, he ran down the stairs, with Jane and Bailey doing their best to keep up.

'What is that thing, Father?' shouted Jane as they raced along a ground-floor corridor, but Sir Christopher could not hear her question for all the rattling that was coming from inside the bucket.

With a great jangling of keys, Bailey ran ahead, opened a side door, and hastily ushered them through. They found themselves in a very hot room with an enormous fireplace that took up a whole wall. The room was filled

with freshly cast bells of all sizes, which were waiting to be hung in the cathedral.

Some of them were huge, weighing close to sixteen tonnes, but it was one of the much smaller bells that Sir Christopher had his eye on.

'Jane, stay close. Bailey, turn that one upside down.'

Bailey did as instructed and turned the small bell upside down and propped it up with some bricks. As quickly as he could, Sir Christopher plunged the bucket into the bell, taking care to keep the monster trapped inside.

'I'll hold the lid in place until you pour in the brass.' Sir Christopher gestured towards the fire. Jane followed Bailey and stared into a pot of molten brass hung above the fire, bubbling away like a volcanic stew. Bailey took the pot from its hook, carried it carefully back and poured the molten brass over the bucket until it was covered completely and the bell was filled to the top.

Sir Christopher pushed over a barrel of water so that it splashed the bell with an almighty hiss of steam.

'More water!' shouted Sir Christopher, and Bailey obliged, pouring bucket after bucket of water on to the

slowly cooling metal. When the steam cloud cleared, there was no trace of the strange creature that had been trapped inside the bell.

Forty-five minutes later, Jane stood at the docks on the River Thames holding her father's hand and squinting into the rising sun.

'Where is the ship going?' asked Jane as she watched sailors release the ropes that tethered an enormous ship to the jetty.

'Greece. Spain. Then Italy, I believe. A trading ship like this will visit a great many ports before it returns. But I have given the captain orders to hurl that bell into the ocean once he is well clear of England.'

'Did you tell him what was hidden inside it?'

'What do you think?' said Sir Christopher, looking quizzically at his daughter.

'Oh. Of course you didn't. It will be our secret.' She squeezed his hand, and they both turned to walk back to the carriage where Bailey and his horses were waiting to take them home.

But the captain never had the chance to carry out Sir Christopher's orders because just a week after setting sail, a terrible storm sent the ship, its entire crew and the bell containing the abomination of Master Buzzard to the bottom of the Mediterranean Sea, and there it remained undiscovered . . .

. . . Until last Friday.

NELLY-SON

LONDON. FRIDAY. JUST AFTER LUNCH . . .

Nelson Green stood on the school sports field completely frozen with panic. The reason Nelson was standing on the sports field was that he was one of twenty-two boys in the midst of a game of rugby. And the reason Nelson was frozen in panic was because he was standing between the touchline and the ball, which was being carried by a short, stocky and furiously determined boy called Ravi Moyse from the opposite team. The correct thing for Nelson to do here would be to tackle Ravi, but he was so afraid of making yet another mistake that he just closed his eyes and did nothing. The howls of outrage and frustration from his teammates completely drowned out the cheers of other team as Ravi scored.

Nelson's team sank to their knees in despair or stared at the ground to avoid looking at their delighted opponents, some of whom had stopped cheering Ravi and were running over to pat Nelson on the back for making it all possible.

Everyone on Nelson's team knew there was no chance of winning now. They were out of the tournament and just had to play out the last horrible seconds of the game and endure the smug expressions on their opponents' faces.

The whistle blew, the ball was flying, and the teams scattered. Not content with their last try, the opposing team were determined to steal one more before their inevitable victory.

Nelson felt a hard thump to the back of his right shoulder. One of his teammates, the lanky-limbed runny-nosed Jason Boyle, had just bumped into him.

'Sorry, mate,' said Jason, but Nelson knew it wasn't an accident that they had collided. Jason had gone out of his way to bump into him.

Jason wasn't the only one.

Two more of Nelson's teammates barged into him before the smallest and toughest kid on their team, Dean Farah, succeeded in knocking Nelson to the ground.

'Sorry, mate. Didn't see ya there,' said Dean, before sniffing loudly, spitting on the ground and jogging away.

Nelson knew it was pointless trying to keep his emotions under control now. Anger and shame were radiating from every part of him, and he knew that somewhere seven of his most peculiar friends would be picking up the signal loud and clear . . .

A boy on Nelson's team called Daniel Chase had managed to take possession of the ball and was running as fast as his noodle-legs would carry him, but the opposition were closing ranks. As they swooped on Daniel and dragged him to the ground, Daniel let the ball fly out of his hands and it was snatched out of the air by Dean Farah. Dean sprinted forward, but a set of fierce blond twins knocked him off his feet. Once again the ball was flying, and this time it was Jason Boyle who caught it. Pulling it tightly to his chest, Jason charged forwards, but the sight of his ferocious opponents struck him like a lightning bolt of panic, which is why he didn't even look at who he was throwing the ball to. By the time Jason was being crushed into the mud by several players from the opposite team, the ball had landed in the grasp of the worst player on the pitch.

Time is a funny old thing, and, for Nelson, the split second he caught that ball seemed to stretch out before him like chewing gum. In that one brief moment, he saw Daniel Chase looking up from the mud with a horrified expression. He saw the referee looking at his watch and put the whistle to his lips. And when Nelson turned, he saw Ravi charging bull-like towards him. Nelson closed his eyes and braced himself for impact. This time he was holding the ball, which meant it was going to hurt a lot. But at least then it would be over – they would be out of the tournament and he would never have to play rugby again.

SPLAT! A body slammed into the custard-thick mud, but when Nelson opened his eyes he found that it was not his body that had fallen in the mud, but Ravi's. And what was even more surprising was that Ravi was still skidding on his stomach through the mud at high speed. While Nelson's eyes had been closed, every player on the pitch had seen something incredible: Ravi had appeared to

dive towards Nelson but then suddenly change direction in mid-air and shoot across the pitch. The whistle fell out of the referee's mouth as Ravi slid past him like a human torpedo, and the stunned silence that followed was broken by a loud and rasping voice that Nelson knew only too well.

'Run, Nelly-son! Run!'

Standing where Nelson should have been lying was a fat little creature. His skin was bubblegum pink, black caterpillar-thick eyebrows arched over his eager eyes, a pair of stick-thin arms waved enthusiastically, and from his great smiling mouth hung a purple tongue as big and flappy as freshly caught haddock. It is my great pleasure to introduce you to one of Nelson's seven peculiar friends,

invisible to everyone but him: his name is Nosh and, as you can see, he is a monster.

'Run wiv dat ball fing, Nelly-son! Run, run, run!'

Nelson wasn't sure running was going to help, but he could hardly stand there and have a conversation with a monster in the middle of the pitch, could he? Especially as no one else in the world could see it.

And so Nelson ran.

'Ha haaa! Go, go, Nelly-son!' cheered Nosh.

It was as if someone had flipped a switch and all the stunned players on the pitch were suddenly back in action (apart from Ravi, who was busy spitting grass and snorting the mud out of his nostrils). Nelson hugged the ball tight under one arm and ran as fast as he could. Four players from the opposite team came rushing towards him. There was no way of getting past them, so Nelson did something you should avoid doing at all costs in rugby, and that is to run back towards your own goal posts.

That's when Nelson saw them. The rest of his monsters were standing on his goal line yelling and cheering him on. There was Spike, the one who looks like a bright green cactus, but for whom there is never a bright side; and there was Stan, the red one with tiny hooves, purple horns and huge fists, who was permanently on the lookout for a fight. Next to him was Miser, a greedy, blue, egg-shaped pickpocket with arms like octopus tentacles and a pair of shifty bulbous eyes; Puff, a lazy, fluffy, purple, cat-like monster who was half asleep most of the time; and Hoot, a great golden bird with a solid silver beak who was as stupid as he was vain. Last of all was Crush, a bright orange cross between a puppy, a tiny elephant and an air horn. He may have been the smallest of the monsters, but

he was by far the loudest. 'HOOOOONK!' Though it was the only sound he was capable of making, it was clear that Crush meant nothing but support for his beloved Nelson.

'I say! Shouldn't you be running the other way, Master Nelson?' cried Hoot in a voice you would expect from a jolly member of the royal family. And though Hoot was right for a change, Miser had a different perspective.

'Pay no attention to the bird! Continue this way, Master Nelson! Do not stop running!'

'Yeah! Keep comin'! We'll take care of this lot for ya!' said Stan, who had clearly understood Miser's intentions and was now eager to join in the fun.

Nelson didn't need to look over his shoulder because he could hear the stampeding feet and panting breath of the other team. They were hell-bent on bringing him down in the goal zone and claiming an even greater victory.

The monsters parted to allow Nelson through before closing ranks. WHAM! The opposing players appeared to hit an invisible wall and bounce backwards through the air.

'Well don't just stand there! Run back the other way,' said Spike, and Nelson did just that.

'Yeaaaah! You better run fast, Nelly-son!' Nosh was waving and wobbling about among the other players, and though Nelson really did try, he couldn't help feeling like his legs just didn't want any part of this.

'HOOONK!' came the sound of Crush, who was running after Nelson as fast as he could.

The monsters were so excited at this stage that even the laziest monster of all, Puff, couldn't help but become swept up in the moment and cheer, 'Wooo-hooo!'

'Pass it! Pass it to me, Greenie!' yelled Dean Farah with his arms open ready to catch the ball. 'Pass it, you idiot!'

'Shut it, ya berk!' snapped Stan as he barged Dean out of the way.

Nelson didn't see Dean crashing into the ground; he was only concerned with the two blond twins heading towards him. Nelson made a sudden left turn and then, just as quickly, he turned hard right, which resulted in splitting the twins apart. Nelson aimed for the tiny space created between them and ran as fast as he could. His head was down, the ball

hugged tight to his chest with one arm while the other arm pumped the air in time with his legs. As he passed between the twins, he felt the snag of arms around his waist and suddenly he was falling forwards. He hadn't been fast enough and he was going down when he felt a tugging sensation behind his shoulders and his shirt tighten around his chest. Instead of hitting the ground, Nelson was dragged the last few metres to the goal line by Hoot, who flew above him, rugby shirt clenched in his claws, and dropped him face down in the mud.

The whistle blew and Nelson rose from the mud to see the other team lying scattered and bewildered. Daniel Chase's mouth opened so wide that his gum shield popped out. Everyone on Nelson's team cheered. The monsters wanted nothing more than to lift their beloved Nelson into the air and carry him like a hero, but a boy floating in mid-air would have looked very weird.

A final kick of the ball over the goal posts from Jason Boyle did it. Nelson's team were through to the finals. The sports teacher blew his whistle, and the players began jogging off the pitch towards the changing rooms.

'Guys, this is a total, massive disaster,' whispered Nelson to his gathering monsters.

'What you talkin' about?!' asked Stan.

'I'll tell you exactly what I'm talking about—'

But Nelson couldn't finish his sentence because the sports teacher had blown his whistle and was calling to Nelson.

'Let's get going, Green!'

'Yes, sir! Just tying my laces,' shouted Nelson, and he quickly bent down to pretend he was doing just that. 'We can't talk here. I'll get changed and meet you behind the bins at the back of the canteen in a few minutes. And please don't do anything to get me into more trouble between now and then.'

'Well, you 'eard 'im,' said Stan. 'Let's go and wait for 'im. And, Nosh, if you so much as take a nibble of what's inside them bins, I will kick your pink butt right over them goal posts!'

THE MESS WE'RE IN

Nelson had left the changing room and dashed around the back of the school to the bin area in record time by skipping the showers. Right now, muddy knees and elbows were the least of his worries.

'I told the others we shouldn't have come to help you.' Spike sighed as Nelson checked no one was watching and crouched in front of his monsters between two huge bins. 'I said, "Nelson told us to leave him alone until he's back in the school's 'good books'" . . .'

'Forgive us, Master Nelson, but we felt your deep anger and shame,' said Miser.

'Tell me about it. It felt 'orrible,' moaned Spike, and he would have continued to moan had Stan not interrupted.

'What are you apologizing for, Miser? 'E wouldn't 'ave won that game without us!'

Crush gave a sharp 'HONK!' in agreement.

'Look, I know you think you were doing the right thing, but I didn't really want to win,' said Nelson.

'Bah! What ya talkin' about? Course ya did!' barked Stan.

'You are the hero of the match, dear boy! The

champion! Although, I think we can agree a great deal of that was down to me,' crowed Hoot.

'Shush. I'm not a hero. And now I have to play again in the finals.'

'The finals! Well we are gonna knock 'em dead! We're gonna slay those suckers! Tell me what school they're from, and I'll check 'em out. Find out who their weakest players are. Ha ha! Great stuff!' Stan clapped his huge hands together and bared his sharp little teeth in a lopsided grin.

Nelson couldn't help laughing. 'No, Stan. It's not *great stuff*. Everyone on my team hates me, and I don't blame them. I'm rubbish at rugby.'

'Nelly-son not rubbish! Naaah! Nelly-son runnin' faaaaaaast!'

'Nosh, I only volunteered for rugby cos my mum thought it would look good on my school report. I never thought I'd get on the actual team.'

Ahh, the dreaded report.

The summer holiday had been a joyous riot, but arriving at school with invisible monsters in tow had been a disaster that would make any teacher's head spin.

To be fair to Nelson, none of the catastrophes were his fault. The only reason he had fallen through the roof of the school canteen and into the cheese and onion pie was because he'd been trying to pull Nosh out of one of the extractor vents on the roof (Nosh had become stuck while inhaling the smell of the food cooking below).

What happened to George Griffiths wasn't Nelson's fault either. Yes, Nelson had been bullied by George, but it was Stan who had hung George up by his underpants over the stage and left 'Loser' by Beck playing loudly on loop.

When the head teacher's computer was found at the bottom of the swimming pool, CCTV footage showed Nelson carrying the computer into the pool area. What the cameras didn't see was that Nelson was attempting to pull the computer out of his monsters' hands while trying

to explain that they could NOT get rid of his report from the head teacher's computer by drowning it in the pool! (Yes, Nelson's monsters really could be that stupid.)

The list of disasters went on and on, which is why after

several warnings and a meeting with his teachers and parents, it was agreed that Nelson had one more chance to put things right or he would be at serious risk of being expelled.

'Look, I really, really don't wanna be in any more trouble, and if we don't sort out this mess we're in, I might have to go to another school – a special school.'

'Special school, eh? Well, I like the sound of this. You deserve something special, dear boy! The kind of school that looks like a castle. A place where top hats and mustard-coloured knickerbockers are uniform.'

'No, Hoot. That's not what a special school is. I just wanna stay here and I want everything to stop being mad for a bit. We all had a wicked summer, the best summer of my whole life, and we will have loads more fun again, I promise. But right now I need you all to stick to the plan and stay out of my life until my probation ends next Friday.'

Nelson looked at his monsters. Though they were all very different, each monster had the same mournful look in their eyes. Like Nelson, they found having to live apart just awful and they were longing to go back to the fun times.

The school bell rang. Nelson grabbed his backpack and swung it over his shoulders.

'Sorry.' Nelson jogged away, head bowed low to hide the little tears that had sprung from his eyes.

Crush ran after Nelson honking desperately, but Miser

snatched him back with a whip-crack of his tentacles.

'Let Master Nelson go,' said Miser, and Crush gave a very sad 'HONK' as Nosh patted his head.

'S'OK, Crush. Nelly-son sayin' it's gonna be all fun again soon,' said Nosh, before taking a bite out of a very green potato he had found under a bin.

'Yeah, but only if we all stay outta trouble,' groaned Spike.

The others fell silent. They knew only too well that staying out of trouble was pretty much impossible, and as if to prove the point, Nosh's belly ignited – roasting the green potato he'd just eaten, and the jet of flames that roared from his head melted the side of the wheelie bin.

THE EXTRAORDINARY RESIDENTS OF LONDON ZOO

Later that same Friday afternoon, the 274 bus pulled up outside London Zoo, and Nelson's seven monsters got off. When I say 'got off', I mean jumped off the roof of the bus and on to the bus shelter. It was always easier to ride on the roof than risk sitting inside during busy times, where they were likely to bump into someone who might then run from the bus screaming they'd just been touched by a ghost.

'Ah!' Nosh exclaimed after taking a great sniff of air. 'It's feedy time for da penga-wins! I'm a smellin' dem lummy fishes!' He wobbled quickly past the visitors at the entrance and made his way down the path, taking care not to bump into anyone.

Since their separation from Nelson had begun, London Zoo had become the monsters' second home. You might not think of a zoo as being an ideal place to spend the night, let alone weeks, but then again, you are probably not a monster. Though Nelson's monsters thrived in his company and would always prefer to be closer to him than anywhere else, London Zoo did offer some creature comforts to take their minds off the dull ache they felt from having to living apart. For one thing, London Zoo offered a variety of animal enclosures to suit each monster.

The Fruit Bat Forest suited Miser's preference for

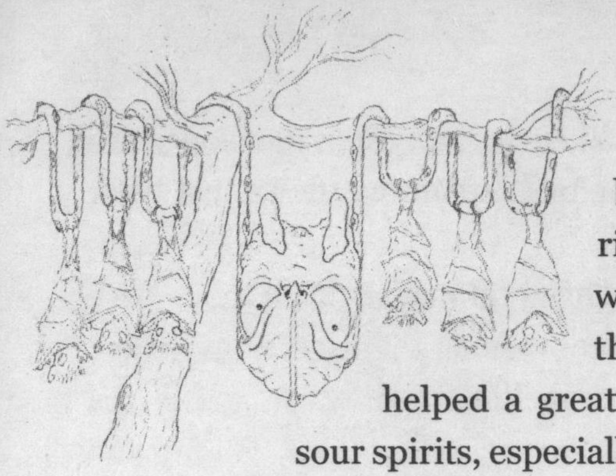

darkness, and the fruit bats knew some terrific ghost stories. The warmth and humidity of the butterfly enclosure helped a great deal in lifting Spike's sour spirits, especially as the butterflies had gentle sing-songy voices and only ever had nice things to say. Puff had become pals with the tigers, who enjoyed sleeping in a huddle as much as he did. Stan found a group of grumpy yaks who enjoyed butting horns and discussing which animals they could easily beat in a fight. Crush would snuggle up each night with the gorillas, who took it in turns to cuddle him like a bed toy. Hoot would perch among the birds living in the gigantic aviary and talk about himself until they were all bored to sleep. And Nosh hung out wherever food was being served, whether it was the elephant house, the aquarium or, at this particular moment in time, the penguin pool.

It was Stan who first realized that not

only was he visible to the yaks, he could also understand what they were moaning about. Wasps from a nearby nest had been bothering them, so Stan helped the yaks out by punching the wasp nest into oblivion. The yaks were very grateful, and over several nights, the other monsters found they too could 'tune in' to what the animals were saying. Spike found he could even talk with the tropical plants and trees, though they spoke very slowly and rarely wanted to talk about anything other than the weather. Being able to communicate and be seen by the animals meant the monsters suddenly had companions galore, and this at least made living apart from Nelson a little less gloomy.

'I shall see you on the morrow, my fine fellows!' Hoot flew off towards the aviary leaving Miser, Stan, Spike, Crush and Puff beneath the sign post directing them to their favourite areas.

'There's no point in me going to the butterfly house until closing time. It's too busy in there at the moment,' moaned Spike.

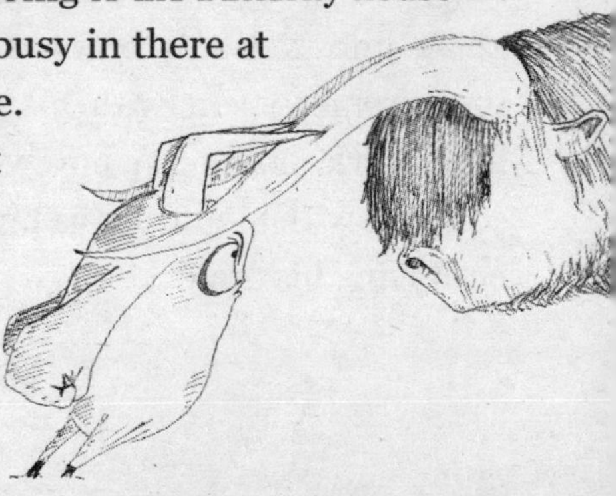

A couple walked past them pushing a buggy with a sleeping child inside it. The couple sat down on the bench, and as the mother squeezed a packet of pulped apple and carrot into her child's mouth, her phone slipped out of her back trouser pocket and on to the ground. Miser felt that hot surge of temptation rush through his tentacles. He wanted so much to snatch the phone and stash it within the folds of his skin with all his other 'treasures', but remembered that Nelson had forbidden stealing.

'May I suggest we visit the camels to pass the time? They know some very amusing jokes. Especially Gerti,' suggested Miser.

'Can someone carry me?' said Puff. 'I'm too tired to walk any more today.'

But of course none of them had any intention of carrying the lazy rotter.

Stan chuckled. 'I 'eard Gerti tells some well rude jokes.'

And without saying anything, the rest of the monsters had already started walking towards the camel enclosure. Nothing cheers up a monster quite like a camel joke.

On the other side of London, Nelson sat in his bedroom. His homework was spread out on his bed, but the pages might as well have been blank, for not one word was going into Nelson's brain. He was lost in thoughts of the summer spent with his monsters, and none of his homework, no matter how vital it was to take in, could compete with memories as fantastic as the ones currently occupying his mind.

Like the time he and his monsters had been sharing a pizza on the roof of the local swimming pool and had noticed a young man on the street below steal a woman's purse from her handbag. The thief had been swift, but upon Nelson's instruction, Miser had picked the thief's pocket and replaced the woman's purse in her bag as she got into her car and drove away. Nelson and his monsters had loved seeing the confused face of the pickpocket when he realized the purse had gone, and from that day on, Miser found he got just as much pleasure picking pickpockets' pockets as he did picking pockets himself. (Apologies if reading this line out loud has put your tongue in a twist.)

In an effort to get his mind back on the lousy business of homework, Nelson took a deep breath and shook his head. It didn't work. Another memory had popped up to say hello.

This one was of sitting in a tree in the park at night watching Hoot perform an aerial dance routine to music playing on a portable speaker. (He had chosen *Equinoxe* by Jean-Michel Jarre, if you must know.) Nelson had laughed so much, he had fallen out of the tree, only to be caught by Puff. This memory was shoved aside by one Nelson loved the most. It was of bedtime in his tent. There was no way his monsters could stay with him in the house, but Nelson's parents had agreed that Nelson could sleep in the tent in the garden while the weather was warm. Crush was snuggled next to him, the other

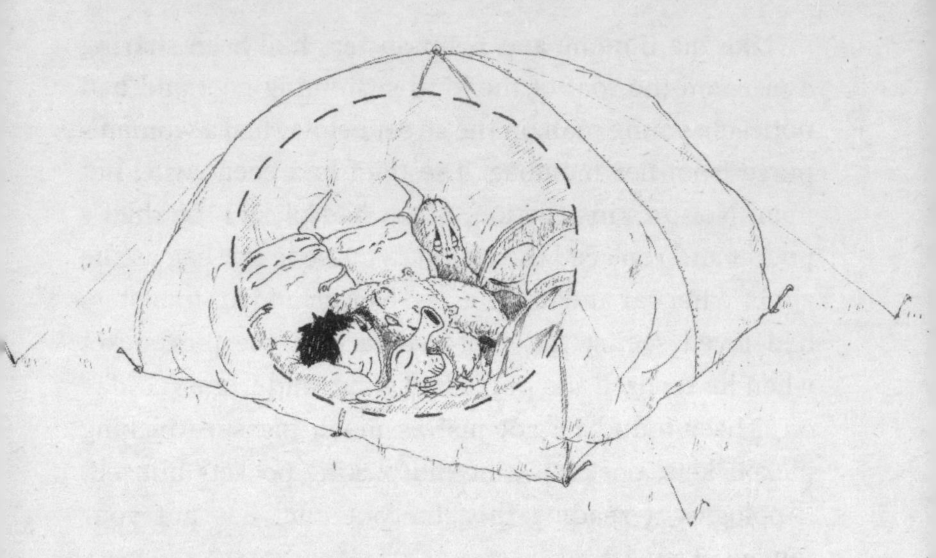

monsters crowded around his bed snoring and wheezing, and Puff spread out on top of Nelson's duvet, purring like a giant cat and emitting a faint scent like lavender mixed with vanilla through his fur that put them all into a sleep as deep as space.

It was no use. The homework was never going to win against memories like these. When Nelson was with his monsters, his thoughts were clear and un-muddled and his energy levels were turned up to ten; but whenever he was apart from his monsters, he couldn't think straight, and his energy levels dropped through the floor. It was like that feeling you have when you've watched way too much TV in the middle of the day and your brain feels so unloved it goes on strike.

The good news for Nelson and his monsters was that

this period of separation was only a few days away from coming to an end.

The bad news was that Nelson's life was not going to get better. In fact, it was about to get a lot worse and, according to a seagull called Edna that had just arrived at London Zoo, very scary indeed.

A SEAGULL WITH VERY BAD NEWS

Edna was a large, wild seagull, generally regarded by the birds in the London Zoo aviary as 'nice, but a bit of a gossip'. However, at this moment in time, she could barely speak for being so exhausted.

'Give the poor dear some space,' said Hoot, even though he was the only one next to her, as the rest of the birds were inside the netted aviary.

Edna closed her eyes. If her heart had been a drum, then it was gradually slowing down from a hardcore techno beat to smooth R&B. The news she had to share was extremely urgent, which is why she had flown all the way from the south coast of England without stopping once. Edna had been enjoying a weekend of diving into the sea and catching fish when she met her old friend Carlos (also a seagull and, if she was honest, one she found very attractive indeed). Carlos had just flown all the way from Greece to share some terrible news with her.

'An evil thing,' wheezed Edna, and all of the birds in the aviary fell silent.

'An evil thing, eh? In the sea? And your friend Carlos the seagull, he saw this evil thing, did he?'

‘No. The fish. The fish in the sea told Carlos it is trapped inside a shipwreck.’

‘I see. And where might this shipwreck be?’ asked Hoot.

‘I just told you! South of a Greek island called Syros.’

‘Well then, there’s nothing to worry about! My dear Edna, Greece is very, very far away! Now, I think a little dinner might do us all the world of good, don’t you?’

Edna squawked angrily and Hoot realized that he might have failed to see the urgency in the matter.

‘Very well, Edna. Do go on.’

‘The fish of Syros say there’s something evil hidden inside the shipwreck, and some humans plan to raise the

evil thing to the surface. And when they do, the end will be upon us all!'

At this, all the birds fell silent. Edna closed her eyes and took a deep breath before continuing.

'The fish insisted this message be passed on to your human friend, the boy called Nelson. See, they believe he has a connection to the people planning to rob from the shipwreck.'

Fish insisting on anything is quite an odd thing to hear about, but their specific request that Nelson help them save the world may seem odder still. You see, ever since Nelson saved a group of fish from a poisoned spring in Brazil, word got out of his good deed and he had become legendary in the fish community, who until then were only used to being caught and either put into tanks or eaten by humans.

'Well go on then,' said Hoot, who was becoming increasingly fed up about losing the spotlight to this overtly theatrical seagull.

'You've gotta pass the fish's message on to Nelson. They said Nelson knows two of the men – one with green hair like a parrot, and the other with only one leg. Nelson must tell them *not to take the evil thing out of the ocean.*'

'Now, those descriptions do ring a bell. Though I'm not sure why. But are you quite sure about this evil thing, Edna? Because if we're all being honest, dear, you do have a reputation for exaggerating.' Hoot was keen that this all be a mistake, but Edna shook her head.

'Me? Exaggerate! I've never heard anything so ridiculous in my entire life! Fish never lie and neither does my darling Carlos, and they made it very clear – if this thing escapes, it will be the end of us all. So go to your friend before it's too late!' Though she had hardly caught her breath, Edna took to the sky once more and joined the flocks of birds flying north.

The other birds inside the aviary were hopping about and squawking nervously.

'Right. Well, I must say Edna's put a bit of dampener on the afternoon, hasn't she? Even so, I should probably alert the others, just in case what she said really is important. Though I highly doubt it. Silly seagull.'

Hoot flew off towards the camel enclosure where he could hear his fellow monsters laughing their heads off at one of Gerti's jokes.

TRUTH AND DUMPLINGS

'You're gonna love the dumplings here – they're amazing,' said Celeste, who had just ordered for both herself and her younger brother Nelson. 'Oh, by the way, well done with the rugby. Mum said your team went through to the final today.'

'Was this was all Mum's idea?' asked Nelson as he peeled the paper off his plastic chopsticks. 'Coming here for dinner, I mean.'

'I'm not gonna start lecturing you, if that's what you think. And no, it wasn't Mum's idea. It was mine. I just thought you looked like you needed a break from the homework, Mr Moody Pants.'

Nelson couldn't help but smile at her babyish insult.

'Well, you are moody,' said Celeste as she began to pour jasmine tea for Nelson. 'Now, could Mr Moody Pants please try some of this tea and tell me why he's been so flipping distant these last few weeks?'

It was a fair enough question. He had not been himself for the last few weeks. He'd been anxious and swinging between all kinds of moods except the good ones. He would have begun biting his nails again, but there was nothing left to bite.

'It tastes like soap,' said Nelson sipping tea from a tiny cup without handles.

'Bzzz! Don't change the subject. Minus five points for that,' said Celeste, just as the waiter arrived and loaded their table with delicious plates of food.

'Look, I know Mum and Dad have been on at you lately, but it's only because they care and they don't know what's going on with you. I mean they don't want you to be expelled.'

'I told Mum and Dad, I'm gonna work harder, OK? I've got that exam on Monday, and I promised I would pass it.'

'You're not upset because I've been spending so much time with Ivan, are you?'

Celeste has got a boyfriend called Ivan, but don't worry, you'll like him. He's kind right down to his bones, smells of freshly washed clothes, and he's handsome in that scruffy surfer kind of way, but he instantly won Nelson's approval for two reasons: 1) Ivan rides everywhere on a bike that he put together himself; and 2) Ivan is deaf, so he and Celeste mainly communicate with each other using sign language, and Nelson cannot help but find this impressive.

'No. No, I like Ivan. He's cool. And he's been teaching me some sign language.'

'Then what is it, Nelse? What's up with you?'

Where on earth was Nelson to begin? Well, obviously things began to go very wrong indeed when Celeste – his big sister, his guardian angel, and the glue that held his crazy family together – had been kidnapped and held captive in Brazil by their auntie Carla. Then, while his family searched for Celeste, Nelson had been left with his uncle Pogo, and that's when things got even more crazy. Uncle Pogo had taken Nelson to work with him, which happened to mean fixing the plumbing at St Paul's Cathedral, and it was there, on a stormy night, that Nelson had tripped and fallen on Sir Christopher Wren's secret sin-extracting machine. Trouble was, the sins it extracted from Nelson took on a life of their own and became the seven monsters you just met on the rugby pitch.

'If I tell you what's wrong, you'll just think I've gone nuts.'

'You already are nuts. Everyone in our family is nuts. Nice nuts, though. You know, like chocolate-covered almond nuts.' Celeste began dishing out rice into their bowls.

It may have been the jasmine tea or maybe that he just didn't have the strength to hold on to such a big secret any more, but for the first time since the seven monsters came into his life, Nelson found himself ready to tell his sister the truth. Well, maybe just a little piece of the truth to start with. He bit gently into his bottom lip and began to contemplate where to begin.

'Ooh, look at that,' said Celeste staring past Nelson's left shoulder. 'It's like they're all looking at you.'

Nelson turned to see what Celeste was talking about

and discovered seven tropical fish staring at him from the neon-lit aquarium. Nelson quickly turned away and began to dig at his rice with the chopsticks.

'That's so weird! They're totally eyeballing you,' said Celeste with a chuckle before tucking into her food.

Being stared at by fish wasn't weird for Nelson though.

Fish of all kinds noticed him and responded to him as if he were some kind of hero, and while it is nice to be thought of as a hero, it is also very awkward. Especially when you are sitting with your big sister in a Chinese restaurant about to tell her the biggest, most unbelievable secret of all time.

'If you don't start telling me the truth, I get to eat all the dumplings,' said Celeste, slurping on some noodles.

'OK. Well . . . uhh . . . I've got . . . I've got monsters, Cel.' Nelson looked up at his sister for a reaction, but she remained composed and appeared to be completely open to whatever he was going to say next.

Maybe Celeste would believe him. Maybe he really didn't have to bear the weight of this extraordinary secret all by himself. The thought of sharing his secret with his

sister was suddenly so appealing that the truth came pouring out of him. 'Actual, real-life monsters. Seven of them. One for each of the seven deadly sins. Seriously, they're about as tall as this table. Well, one of them's a bit smaller. And they're all different-looking, but . . . but no one can see them or hear them. Except me, obviously. And I suppose they're like my friends, yeah, they are my friends – my best friends, it's just that they've been getting me into loads of trouble since we got back to school . . .'

Nelson paused in order to gauge whether his sister believed what he has said so far.

'Well, go on. What kind of trouble?'

'Like that time when the police came to school cos they found Mr Hamilton the geography teacher on the roof.'

'Oh yeah. That was weird. Wasn't he asleep inside his fishing boat on the roof?'

'Exactly!'

'But you didn't do that.'

'No, but my monsters stuck him and his boat up there.'

'OK,' said Celeste slowly. 'And why did your *monsters* do that?'

'Cos Mr Hamilton had made me feel bad in class the day before. He was all, like –' and at this point Nelson put on a nasal man's voice to mimic his teacher – '"None of you have any sense of adventure these days. No *gumption*. You know when I was your age, my friends and I took the headmaster's motorbike apart, it was a Triumph, beautiful bike it was, and we reassembled it on the roof of the school." And then Mr Hamilton turned to me and said, "Judging by his gormless expression, I don't think Nelson here even knows what the word 'gumption' means," and everyone laughed at me. And that was it. I got this feeling in my stomach like being angry and embarrassed all at once, and my monsters felt it too. They feel everything I do.'

'And they were with you? In class?'

'No! No, they were in the school playground at the time. It's a nightmare if they come into class with me. Have you seen that big bite taken out of the tire swing? That was Nosh.'

'Uhhh . . .'

'He's the hungry one – you know, greed. Anyway, what I'm saying is they feel the same things I do. Wherever they are. And Mr Hamilton had made me feel, well . . . ashamed and stupid. So that night, they decided to get back at Mr Hamilton. They carried him out of his house while he was asleep and stuck him in his boat on the roof of the school.'

Celeste took a deep, steadying breath. She certainly hadn't been prepared for a story like this.

'Puff, he's the lazy one, he can fart this kind of sleeping gas, which is how they got Mr Hamilton on the roof without him waking up.' Nelson chuckled. It had begun to feel exhilarating to talk to his sister about his monsters, and he couldn't stop now. 'I didn't ask them to do it – they just thought it would make me feel better. You see,

they get carried away. They can't stop themselves doing mad stuff.' Nelson crammed a dumpling into his mouth. The lightness of letting go of his secret had made him extremely hungry.

Celeste looked up at the fish, who were still staring at Nelson as if they were as surprised by his story as she was.

'And . . . I suppose it was these monsters that dropped you through the canteen roof?'

'Yes! Well, they didn't mean to. We were all trying to get Nosh out of the air vent – like I said, he's the greedy one. He'd got stuck while he was sniffing the food smells and . . . Are you OK, Cel?'

Celeste's eyes had begun to glisten with tears and she took a sharp, shuddering breath.

'Cel? What's wrong?'

'Nothing, it's just . . . Listen, me being kidnapped, that was a really, really horrible thing for us all to go through.' Her voice weakened from trying to keep her tears at bay. 'And sometimes when people experience something as traumatic as that, it's natural for them to find ways or, you know, invent ways to cope, and *there's nothing wrong with it*.'

Celeste didn't believe him.

He'd finally told her the truth, and she thought he was making it all up.

'But I didn't invent them, Cel. They're not imaginary friends; they're real.'

People on the tables either side of them looked at Nelson, who lowered his voice and leaned towards Celeste.

'Honestly. They helped me rescue you in Brazil. It was

us that found you in that jungle, but I never said anything cos I thought you wouldn't believe me then.'

Even Nelson had to admit it sounded ridiculous now. He lay his chopsticks on the table in defeat. Celeste reached out and grabbed his hand.

'All right, all right. Let's say that's true. These monsters, these friends of yours, they happened to appear when I went missing, right?'

'Yeah . . . but that's only because I was helping Uncle Pogo with a leak at St Paul's and I fell on—' Nelson had stopped mid-sentence because of a very loud and very familiar honking sound. Not a bicycle horn or a car horn, but the unmistakeable 'HONK' of his little monster called Crush.

Nelson spun around, and sure enough Crush was running towards him at top speed, zigzagging between the legs of the chairs, tables and waiters.

'Nelson? You all right?' asked Celeste.

'Crush is here! He's one of my monsters!' Nelson reached out to grab Crush, but Crush dodged Nelson and ran right past, honking loudly.

'HONK! HOOOONK!'

'Crush? Crush! Come back!' Nelson jumped up and hurried after his little monster. 'I'll bring him right back, Cel.'

Crush turned a corner leading to the toilets, and Nelson ran after him, leaving Celeste on her own and very confused indeed.

Nelson burst through the toilet door, nearly knocking out a man on his way out. 'Sorry!' he gasped, but he was too busy looking for Crush to hear the man's curse.

'Honk!'

It was Crush and he was inside one of the cubicles. Nelson opened the cubicle door and found Crush standing on top of the water tank. With each of his four arms, Crush pointed up towards a window that was wide open with six monsters peering through it.

MONSTERS IN THE TOILET

'Phwoar!' said Nosh, his face squished between Stan and Hoot. 'Dis toilet stinky nice! Me smellin' soap and fish skins!'

Nelson was standing inside one of the toilet cubicles looking up at the monsters who peered in at him through the window. Someone else had just entered the toilets, so Nelson flushed the loo to hide the sound of his voice.

'Guys! I only told you to stay away a few hours ago,' he whispered, and they all answered him at once. What a noise it was. All those strange voices, rasping, growling, hooting, honking and moaning.

'Stop! One at a time,' whispered Nelson, and Miser took over speaking duties.

'Master Nelson, we have it on good authority that your uncle Pogo and his companion Doody are in grave danger. As are we all.'

'From what? What are you talking about?'

'A very, very evil thing.'

'Oh. OK, I get it. I know what you're doing,' said Nelson, and he sighed. 'Look, making up stories as an excuse to get together isn't going to work, especially right now.'

'Oh no, no, no!' exclaimed Hoot. 'It's no word of a lie, dear boy! Edna was telling me the truth.'

'Edna? Who's Edna?'

'She is a seagull!'

'A *seagull*?'

'He ain't lyin'!' Stan was right to butt in. Hoot was useless at explaining things, especially in a crisis.

'The fish community asked for you specifically, Master Nelson,' said Miser.

'Not *more* fish. They won't leave me alone these days.'

'Well these particular fish seem to think your uncle and his friend may be in Greece.'

'They *are* in Greece; they're filming a TV show. But come on, everyone knows where they are, so don't pretend this is some big deal.'

'The fish described your uncle and his friend perfectly – a man with one leg, and another with green hair like a parrot – and they insisted you warn both men not to take the wicked treasure they are searching for from the sea. If they succeed, a terrible, terrible evil will escape and that will be the end of us all . . .'

But Nelson didn't hear the last few words Miser said as his sister was calling to him from outside the toilets.

'Nelson? You feeling all right?'

Having his monsters close by again allowed Nelson to think more clearly. Now he realized it was madness to have thought his sister would believe him, and even if he did find a way to show his invisible monsters to Celeste, what then? As if his life wasn't already a complete mess, then surely revealing his monsters to her was certain to turn their lives upside down once and for all. It had all been a huge mistake. He had to get out of that toilet, away from his monsters, and set things straight with his sister as quickly as possible.

'Yeah! Be out in a minute, Cel!' Nelson turned back to his monsters and in an urgent whisper said, 'Guys, this is a nightmare. We *can't* meet up any more, OK? Not until I start proving I'm not a total disaster.'

As Nelson flushed the toilet and left the cubicle, he could hear his monsters protesting loudly.

'Call da uncle Pogo, Nelly-son!' cried Nosh.

'Yeah! If this thing is as bad as we think it is, the whole world's gonna cop it!' Stan shouted, and it was the last thing Nelson heard before leaving the toilets.

Back at the table, Nelson finished his food and looked across at his sister, who was still watching the gawping fish.

'I'm sorry if I was a bit weird earlier. You were right. I made up all that stuff about having monster friends. Got carried away, I suppose. Sorry, Cel.'

'You actually had me convinced for a bit there.' Celeste topped up their cups of jasmine tea and smiled. 'I was thinking we should probably get some doughnuts on the way home.'

'Yeah, we should,' said Nelson, smiling back at her.

He was nervous his monsters would be waiting for

him outside the restaurant, but they were nowhere to be seen. They had followed Nelson's orders and gone back to the zoo, and though it was what he had told them to do, it made him feel like crying again.

DOODY INVESTIGATES!

Sometimes bad things happen by surprise. BLAM! You accidentally walked into a glass door you thought was open. Or SPLODGE! You bit into that jam doughnut too eagerly, and now there's a dark stain on your trousers that not only looks as if you peed yourself, it's also attracting wasps! But sometimes bad things creep up slowly, and even though you know they are approaching, there is nothing you can do to escape them. This feeling is called dread. It may be an exam you have in a few weeks, your appointment with the dentist to have a filling put into one of your teeth, or, in the case of Nelson's monsters, believing that an evil creature was about to escape from the ocean and destroy the world. I'm sure they would all have preferred a quick BLAM! or a SPLODGE! or even an OUCH! compared to the dread that swirled around their bellies.

It certainly didn't help that Nelson thought they were making it all up.

Nelson was in his bedroom wearing Stormtrooper pyjamas and trying with all his might to revise for a maths test on Monday when he heard his uncle Pogo's voice coming from downstairs.

Pogo wasn't down there in person. He was on TV; a co-presenter of the six-part TV show *Doody Investigates*, in which Doody (Professor of History John Doodson) tested the inventions and theories left behind by Sir Christopher Wren. Like a sheepdog reacting to his master's whistle, the sound of Uncle Pogo saying '. . . testing out Sir Christopher Wren's sin extractor . . .' made Nelson spring from his chair, dash across the landing and hang the top half of his body over the banister to hear what his uncle was saying.

'. . . the idea being that these needles extract the seven deadly sins from a person's soul . . .'

Now Nelson simply had to see the television. Running downstairs into the living room was not an option as his parents had forbidden watching TV until he showed a dramatic and consistent improvement at school, so, moving as quietly as he could, Nelson dashed into his parents' bedroom to watch the little TV that was perched on top of a set of drawers.

The screen lit up . . . and there was the sin extractor. It looked exactly as it had the night he had fallen on it. Doody was in the British Museum warehouse, explaining to the viewers what they were seeing.

'. . . But although Sir Christopher Wren never recorded anything about this mysterious device, his daughter Jane made note of it in her diaries, and our research team found

mention of an apprentice who worked for Christopher Wren at the time.'

Pogo took over from Doody and lifted a dust sheet that had been covering an oil painting.

'And here he is! This is a portrait of William Buzzard: son of Lord and Lady Buzzard of Norfolk and Sir Christopher's assistant. See what's behind him? That's right – it's the sin extractor!

'According to Jane's diaries, Buzzard was very vain and a bit of a spoilt so-and-so. He only served as Wren's apprentice for a short time, and her father thought he was an idiot. Apparently the only reason Buzzard wanted to work for Sir Christopher was because he thought it would make him famous.'

The picture cut to a close-up of a leather diary with the initials J. W. on the cover, clasped shut by a golden lock. Doody opened the diary, revealing the handwritten pages.

'Yeah, so basically Buzzard planned to become famous by being the first bloke on earth to be completely cleansed of sin. And to do that, he had to lay himself out on this table.'

The camera followed Uncle Pogo as he crouched beneath the table to point at the seven copper vials held in a rack.

'The idea was that Buzzard's sins were to be somehow drained out of him by the needles and collected into these tubes, each representing one of the seven deadly sins. Now, according to Jane, this test *really* did happen and something *really* was extracted from Buzzard. But what we want to know is what exactly came out of him? And is it still out there somewhere?'

Nelson knew exactly what came out, and for the first time it dawned on him that maybe someone else had been through what he had. That someone other than him had made their own set of seven monsters. Would they look and behave the same as his? Would he be able to see them too? Could this be what the fish had warned his own monsters about?

Nelson shook his head. This was no time for thinking; it was time for paying attention!

Doody joined Pogo in crouching by the copper vials, picking one up and examining it as he spoke.

'Jane describes seeing seven living creatures. One was 'bout the size of a chicken, and it ate the other six. Yuck!'

Nelson thought of Nosh . . . but Nosh wouldn't dream of eating his fellow monsters!

'Of course, it's likely this young lady, Jane Wren, had a wild imagination, and none of this really happened. But what if she was telling the truth? What if there really was a creature? Whatever happened, it was bad enough to scare Buzzard to death. Poor bloke fell trying to escape it, leaving this creature thing. Sir Christopher wasn't taking any chances either. He didn't just chuck it in the bin; he trapped it inside a bell and sent it as far away from London as possible. And here's where it gets spooky, folks. The trading ship that took the bell went down in a storm somewhere off the coast of Greece. Not a soul survived, and whatever it was that came out of Buzzard could still be down there, somewhere in the wreck of that ship . . .'

Doody paused, before replacing the copper vial and straightening up.

'After the break, we'll be going beneath the waves,

where Pogo and I hope to recover some seriously spooky treasure . . .'

The picture changed to a torchlit underwater shot of Pogo in full scuba gear pointing towards a barnacle-encrusted bell lying amidst the wreck of the ship.

Theme music began to play, which meant it was time for a commercial break, and Nelson heard the living-room door open. He quickly switched off the TV, hurled the remote towards his mother's pillow and dashed back across the landing into his bedroom.

Nelson loved his uncle Pogo very much and would never want anything bad to happen to him, but the thought of phoning him to say, 'One of those things you are taking out of the sea contains an evil monster and you must put it back,' felt like it would result in yet another member of his family thinking he was making up stories, and he could really do without that right now. Just imagining his uncle asking, 'Who told you about this evil monster?' and his reply being, 'My own monsters heard it from a seagull called Edna, and she heard it from some Greek fish,' sealed Nelson's decision to pull his pillow over his head and do nothing. It was a decision that would turn out to be the worst one of Nelson's life.

THE STORM INSIDE THE TRAIN

It was Saturday night. Twenty-four hours had passed since Doody and Pogo's live deep-sea dive had aired in the UK, and everyone working on the show considered it to be the highlight of the series. As the TGV train they were travelling on hurtled its way through the moonlit French countryside, inside the train all but one of the TV crew dozed comfortably in their cabins.

The wide-awake passenger happened to be Nelson's uncle Pogo, and he could feel his chin being tickled. Doody had fallen asleep with his head resting on Pogo's

shoulder so that Doody's green Mohawk brushed against him.

Opposite them sat Hilary, the director of their TV show, and James, the camera operator. Pogo smiled at how they had all managed to get equally sunburned faces and decided to take a look at the photos on his phone for the third time. He chuckled. There were several photos of the happy crew preparing underwater cameras for the shoot and at least a dozen photos of Pogo's prosthetic leg on to which he had attached an underwater jet. It had felt so good to move with such ease underwater; on land, movement always required a great deal of effort. Pogo couldn't help but imagine how much fun it must be to be a seal (apart from being a shark's favourite snack), but it was nothing compared to the heart-stopping thrill of discovering the shipwreck.

They had recovered 116 individual relics from the wreck, some as large as a cow and some as small as coins. Once they were back in London, they planned to carefully chip away the salty crusts and discover exactly what was beneath, but for now all the relics were just as they had found them and perfectly preserved in frozen containers. The Greek naval ship they had hired had brought them to the south coast of France, where they had loaded their discoveries and themselves on to a high-speed train bound for Paris. From Paris, the plan was to transport everything to London on the Eurostar, but that part of the plan was never going to happen.

The train was suddenly screeching to a halt. Luggage was falling from the overhead racks. A tumbling chaos rippled throughout every carriage. Somewhere a baby started crying. The train driver was saying something over the public address system in French, but no one could hear a word above the passengers' cries of anguish and surprise.

'Whoa! Woss goin' on?' blurted Doody, who had slid off his seat and was now looking up at Pogo from the floor with wide, startled eyes.

'I dunno,' said Pogo, bracing himself against the window and staring out into the night. 'Maybe someone's pulled the emergency break.'

The train shuddered to a stop. Pogo pulled Doody back into his seat and stood up to lower the window. Even though the train was now at a standstill, the outside air rushed into their carriage with tremendous force, whipping anything loose and light into a mini whirlwind. Pogo winced as he turned away from the wind, the skin on his arms bristling with goosebumps, and the temperature inside the carriage dropping from cosy and warm to freezing cold. This was the kind of weather you would expect from the top of a snowy mountain, not the balmy south of France.

'Pogo! Close the window!' called Doody, but Pogo was too busy trying to see what was going on outside to respond.

To his left, Pogo could see the front of the train

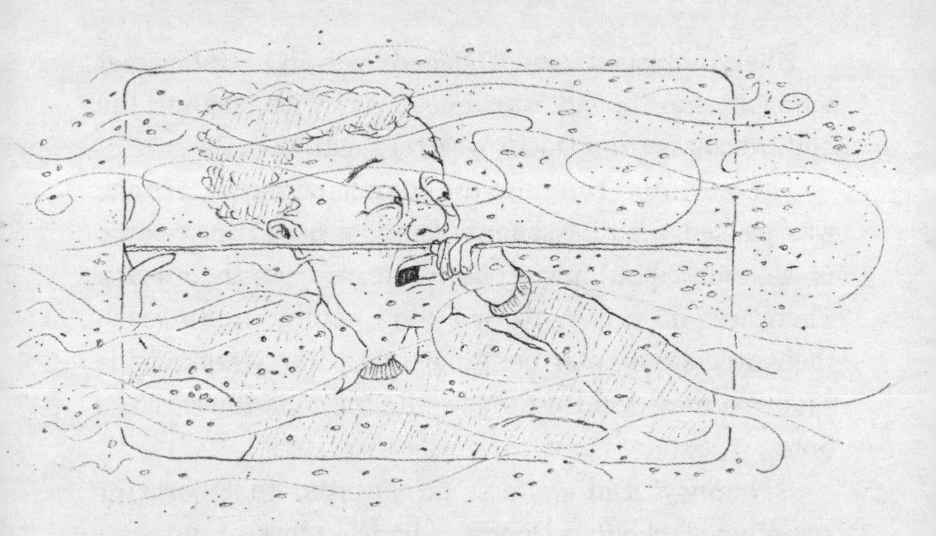

stretching into the distance and three guards clutching their hats to their heads as they ran past his window. Pogo turned to his right to see them running towards another train guard standing on the tracks beside the rear of the train. She was waving a flag furiously and blowing a whistle, though you could barely hear her over the roar of the wind.

'What's with all the arctic wind?' said Doody through chattering teeth.

Pogo closed the window and headed for the door. 'There's something wrong at the end of the train. I'm gonna check our stuff is all right.'

'Hold up, mate! I'll come with ya,' said Doody breathlessly, and then turned to the rest of his TV crew, who sat looking like startled rabbits. 'You lot stay 'ere. Back in a mo. And don't go nickin' my Rolos, Hilary.'

Hilary blushed and nodded guiltily. Until that moment, she thought she'd got away with stealing the odd chocolate from Doody's secret stash.

The corridor running the length of each carriage was packed with passengers flapping about in a panic or moaning about having been thrown from their seats. There was no way Pogo or Doody were going to reach their precious freezer containers in a hurry taking this route, so they decided to leave the train via the carriage door.

'Pheeewy! Did we just get diverted to Siberia or something?' shouted Doody as he tried to keep up with Pogo through the flurry of snow that hit them as they exited the train.

'No! I think we're currently somewhere close to the Dordogne!' (pronounced *Door-doy-n*).

'The Dordogne? Well, remind me to never book a holiday in the Dordogne!'

'This isn't normal weather for round here, Doody! There's something wrong – look!'

Pogo was pointing to the last train carriage that had contained all of the objects they had brought up from the shipwreck. I use the past tense because right now there were pieces of their deep-freeze containers and the relics that had been inside them scattered all over the ground.

'Pogo! It's all smashed up! All of it!'

Doody picked up a broken piece of barnacle-covered metal, but Pogo was way more concerned with what was happening inside the train. Though he had to squint, Pogo could see that where once there had been windows and a door to the carriage, there were now gaping wide holes.

'The snow! It's coming from inside the carriage!' shouted Pogo, leaning into the blizzard and reaching out a hand towards the train.

At that very same moment, a thunderclap erupted from the train. Bolts of lightning shot out from the broken windows, striking nearby trees and bushes and setting them aflame. Pogo and Doody ducked, covering their heads with their arms as a garage-door-sized piece of the train roof was blasted into the air on a fountain of wind and snow. Neither Pogo nor Doody saw the sheet of metal fall from the sky. One moment they were cowering on the train tracks, the next they were both knocked unconscious by the falling debris.

As snowflakes settled on the metal covering Pogo and Doody, and fire continued to lick hungrily at the trees, the vague silhouette of what might have been a dog-sized bird with an oversized and twisted beak sat breathing heavily on what remained of the roof of the train. And what a stench it brought with it. It smelt as if all the bad breath in the world had been brought together to create one foul wind. Some of the passengers had climbed out of the train and were holding their noses as they tried to see what was going on, but to the untrained eye, the creature was invisible, only coming into focus as flakes of snow landed on its outstretched wing, which was pointing north with a trembling claw.

And though none of the passengers could hear it, the creature screamed.

'BUZZAAAAAAAAAAAARD!'

THE SMELL OF FEAR

It was midnight, but as Saturday turned into Sunday, every animal in London Zoo was awake. Every backbone tingled with fear. The monsters felt it too. It was the feeling you get as someone finishes telling you the kind of ghost story that ends with '. . . and they say the ghost still haunts this very room'.

'I say, does this creepy-crawly sensation have something to do with what Edna was on about, or do you think we might all just have a case of the windy pops?' Hoot was always the last to understand what was going on, but Miser put him straight.

'I believe this means Master Nelson did not heed our warning.'

'Oh I bet this means he didn't phone his uncle, doesn't it?! That idiot!' barked Stan.

'HONK!' Crush was defending Nelson, and Stan stepped back. Even Stan wouldn't mess with Crush when he was feeling defensive.

'All right! All right! 'E's my friend too, but if we're honest 'ere, Nelson's probably let us all down big time!'

'Nah, Nelly-son a good boy.' Nosh tried to sound

supportive, but even he couldn't hide his disappointment.

Spike sat down on the ground and looked at his stubby green feet. 'Well, that's it then. There's nothing we can do. Just sit and wait.'

'Yes, now when you say "wait", what exactly are we waiting for?' asked Hoot, but Spike could only shrug. It was Crush who answered Hoot, and though he did not use any words, his low, trembling honk said it all.

'Hoooooooonk.'

As Crush said this, a howler monkey on the other side of the zoo began to howl. It was soon joined by the other howler monkeys, and within just a few seconds every animal in the zoo had joined the awful chorus.

'There! Can you smell that?' Spike was taking repeated sharp sniffs of the evening air. 'It's the smell of fear.'

The other monsters sniffed the air, except for Puff, who was in the midst of an extremely long yawn. He wasn't bored – in fact quite the opposite. He was extremely agitated, and the more anxious Puff felt, the more he yawned.

'Nah! Smells more like leaves and freshly cut grass to me,' said Stan, and he was right. There was a very strong smell, but it was a pleasant smell. The scent of all things green and fresh.

'Nope. The plants and trees and grass give off that scent as a warning to each other.

They're scared. They know something bad is coming. Look.' Spike pointed to the trees that stood around the zoo. They were shedding their leaves. This would be a normal thing to see in the autumn when the leaves were brown and the wind was blowing, but the leaves were still green, and not even a breath of wind could be felt. It looked as if someone had pressed an emergency leaf-release button.

'They're shedding their leaves to protect themselves. They know a big storm's headed this way.' Spike looked through the railings of the zoo into Regent's Park and saw leaves falling from trees everywhere.

'This is nuts! Even the trees know somefing's wrong. I say we go to Nelson's house right now!' said Stan, and the others cheered. Except for Miser.

'No! Master Nelson made it clear! We are NOT to go to him and especially not to his home!'

Stan sighed. 'Then what do ya suggest, eh? We gotta do something!'

'I suggest we contact Master Nelson by some other means.'

'Oh yeah? Like what?' Stan was getting more furious by the second, so Puff stepped into the conversation in order to settle the mood.

'Miser, you know our voices don't work on the

phone. We tried before, remember? That time Crush got locked in the zoo gift shop and we called to ask Nelson what we should do and his mum answered the phone?'

'I remember only too well, which is why I do not suggest we use the telephone.'

'Then what?' said Puff.

'I suggest we confer with Godfrey.'

'Who's Godfrey?' said all of the monsters but Crush.

'Godfrey is a most inventive fruit bat,' said Miser, and with that he turned and ran off towards the enclosure known to London Zoo visitors as Fruit Bat Forest.

GOOD-LUCK CHARM

It was early the next morning. The Sunday sky was headache grey. Nelson followed the smell of bacon to the kitchen where he found his father wearing boxer shorts and an R.E.M. tour T-shirt cooking at the stove while his mother swooshed around in her bright green dressing gown decorating the walls with multicoloured Post-it notes.

'Morning, Nelse. Bacon sarnie?' asked his father as he shoved bacon around the frying pan.

'Uhh . . . yeah. I'd love a sandwich please, Dad,' said Nelson, who had only just realized what his mother was up to. She had written inspirational phrases for Nelson on each Post-it. Before he could protest, she leaped to her own defence.

'I know what you're going to say, but I thought it would just help to put up a bit of extra positive thinking around the place.'

Nelson read one of quotes, this one from Thomas Edison: *Our greatest weakness lies in giving up. The most certain way to succeed is always to try just one more time*. Nelson sighed.

'Listen, I'd go over Niagara Falls in a lunchbox if I thought it would help you get your act together at school,' said his mother, and she stuck the last note on Nelson's forehead.

Nelson rolled his eyes at his dad, who could only offer a shrug and a smile in return. Nelson peeled the note off his head, flopped down into a chair and reached underneath their kitchen table to pet Minty the dog. Minty raised her scruffy little head for a moment before letting it flop back down on the floor. So far, it had been a pretty uneventful weekend for a change. Saturday had passed by without a peep from his monsters, and their warnings of an evil creature being dragged up from the deep by his uncle Pogo had faded away as the weekend rolled on. With a bacon sandwich on the way and a dog asleep at his feet, Nelson felt things were returning to normal.

'Quick! Uncle Pogo's on the telly!' Celeste had just burst into the kitchen, still wearing her pyjamas and looking wild with panic.

'Darling, he's been on the telly for the last four weeks,' said their father as he carried Nelson's sandwich across the room.

'No, not on Doody's show. He's on the news. Right now. He's been in an accident.'

Nelson's father put down the plate and ran, Nelson and his mother following close behind.

Sure enough, there was a photo of Uncle Pogo and Doody on the TV news. The news reporter spoke in an earnest tone that gave Nelson the creeps.

'. . . were struck by debris from an explosion on the train. Doctors have confirmed that both men remain unconscious and are currently being treated for serious multiple injuries . . .'

As the picture changed to images of the train carriage, Nelson was struck by a huge and horrible feeling. It was a stomach-churning cocktail of déjà vu and regret. Here he was, looking at the TV news and seeing *exactly* what his monsters had warned him would happen if he did nothing.

Hilary, the director of Doody's TV show, was being interviewed by the side of the train wreck. She looked lost and confused, her suntan drained from her face, and her eyes red and puffy.

'. . . It's hard to say exactly, but I saw something that looked . . . well, it looked like a sort of storm cloud coming from inside the train . . . It was very dark and there was snow everywhere. Loads and loads of snow and lightning that burned the trees. But the hole in the roof of the train looks like it was made by a creature because there were claw marks all over the metal . . . and the smell, oh it was dreadful . . .'

'*Creature?* Did she just say *creature*?' asked Nelson.

'Shhh!' said his mother. And while the rest of his family continued to listen to Hilary describe what she'd seen, Nelson turned away, the better to focus on recalling the warning from his monsters.

What was it they had said? *A very evil monster trapped at the bottom of the ocean and Uncle Pogo must not raise it to the surface.*

The newsreader moved on to a different story that involved two world leaders shaking hands as their picture was taken, but no one in Nelson's house was listening. As his father rushed to the phone and began making calls to find out which hospital Pogo and Doody had been taken to, Nelson slipped away to his room.

Outside the trees were bare and the pavement ankle-deep with leaves. All over town, dogs (except for Minty) were barking, cats miaowing, and though Nelson couldn't hear them, mice were squeaking, ducks were quacking, and even the ants were yelling their heads off. Birds filled the sky, all flying as fast as they could in the same direction: north. Worms were squirming deeper into the soil. Termites buried deeper into trees. And bats. Yes, there were bats flying up and down his street. He'd never seen bats at night, let alone during the daytime. Every living thing could feel and smell the fear in the air, and the message was clear: something very bad was going to happen.

THUD! Something hit the window, and Nelson jumped backwards and fell on to his bed. THUD! It struck again, and this time Nelson could see it was something soft and grey and nothing to be worried about.

He opened the window and looked down to see Celeste's boyfriend, Ivan, standing on his doorstep.

'Hi, Ivan,' said Nelson.

Ivan waved with his left hand and with his right hand threw something up towards the open window. Nelson caught it and found he was holding a cuddly toy rhino. It was soft and grey and dressed in a white T-shirt with the words 'I'M A WINNER' printed on it.

Ivan signed to Nelson. *It's for you.*

Nelson ran downstairs and opened the door for Ivan.

'What does that sign mean – I can't remember?' asked Nelson, and Ivan replied without his hands, his words sounding softer at the edges than they would for someone with normal hearing.

'It's for you. I won it at the steam fair last night. Thought it might bring you good luck in your tests.'

'Thanks, Ivan.'

'Sorry you've been going through such a hard time at school, mate.'

Nelson shrugged.

'Well done on the rugby.'

Nelson made the sign for '*Thanks*'.

Ivan smiled. 'I need to teach you more sign language.'

'Yes please.'

Celeste appeared, threw her arms around Ivan and kissed him.

'Look what Ivan gave me.' Nelson held up the toy rhino.

'Did you say thank you?'

'Of course I did! Look, can I just ask you something?'

'Yep.'

'What would you do if you'd really let someone down, like something bad happened to them, and you could've done something to help them or stop it ever happening?'

'Depends. Suppose I would tell them I was sorry.' Celeste was already fastening the strap on her cycle helmet.

'What if you couldn't? I mean, what if it was too late to tell them?'

'It's never too late to say sorry. Look, whatever it is you're worried about, Nelson, you can tell me.'

'OK.'

There was a pause before Celeste asked. 'Well, are

you going to tell me?'

'Uh . . . maybe not right now. Is that OK?'

Celeste laughed as she unlocked her bicycle from the fence.

'Yeah. I mean, it's a bit annoying, but yeah, 'course it's OK. Tell me later.'

Nelson nodded.

'See you later, Nelse. And call me if you hear any news about Pogo and Doody!'

Celeste and Ivan rode away on their bikes. Nelson waved, but his mind had already returned to Pogo and Doody.

'She would have done something to help,' Nelson said to himself, and it was true. Given the choice between helping someone and doing nothing, Celeste would always choose to help.

The sound of flapping wings brought Nelson's attention back to the real world, where several bats had suddenly dived out of the sky above his house. This would not have been so alarming had they not been aiming straight towards his front door.

'Aaah!' cried Nelson, pulling the door shut just in time to block the little black bodies from getting inside. *Donk! Donk! Donk!* was the sound of three bats hitting the wood. Why on earth were bats trying to attack him? Was this some kind of punishment for not doing the right thing? There was no sound to suggest they were still outside the door, so Nelson took a peep. The bats were there but flying above his house. As far as bad omens go, this was up there with the worst of them. Nelson climbed the stairs, but in his mind he could still see the bats circling outside.

A VERY FROSTY RIVER RACE

Ever since they were teenagers, it had become a tradition for Matt and Alex to race each other in canoes along the Dordogne river on their annual summer holiday at Alex's grandmother's house. In the early days, the races had just been a lot of splashing about, packed lunches and good fun; but now they were older and had girlfriends, a very competitive edge had crept in.

'Paddle left, Sienna! Left! LEFT!' shouted Matt to his girlfriend, Sienna, who was sat right in front of him and still shivering wet. Actually, it was more like he was shouting *at* Sienna, which is why she slammed her oar down in protest.

'It's just a race, Matthew! Just a stupid race!'

'Would it kill you to at least *try* paddling?' was Matt's (in my opinion, very badly judged) response.

'I am never doing this again! Do you understand? I AM NEVER GETTING IN A CANOE WITH YOU AGAIN!'

The boat began to accelerate as it caught the current taking them around a bend in the river.

'FINE! WITH! MEEEEE!' yelled back Matt at equal volume, and Sienna burst into tears.

'Oh great. Yeah, nice one, Sienna. You just go ahead and cry your eyes out. We're gonna lose for sure now,' moaned Matt, who had forgotten he was recording all of this on a GoPro camera clipped to the top of his helmet. But before Sienna could retaliate, there was a sudden loud bang and the boat jumped a few feet into the air.

Matt and Sienna gasped in shock as their canoe skidded forwards with a hollow scraping sound. What should have been narrow rapids in the river had now frozen solid. The canoe tipped over the edge of the frozen rapids and shot down the ice like a bobsleigh, banging against the rocks either side and making the couple scream. The ice at the bottom levelled out and the canoe was sent spinning like a compass needle across the frozen river.

‘Matt . . . look . . .’ said Sienna in a shaky little voice, and she pointed towards a spectacular wave that had been frozen in a great arc against a large rock on the other side of the river. The most incredible thing about this wave was that it also contained Alex and his girlfriend, Mia. They had both been frozen inside their canoe from the shoulders down, which meant that though they couldn’t move, they could at least breathe. They would have screamed too, but they were all struck dumb by the sight of a glistening creature sitting on the riverbank beside them.

It was lucky for everyone the creature was invisible apart from the sparkling frost that had settled in patches upon its body, for this creature was so frightening and ugly that it would have surely stopped all of their hearts had they caught a glimpse of it. Instead, what they saw resembled a hideous frozen ghost but with no recognizable features. And it stank to high heaven! Well, you can’t spend centuries at the bottom of the sea, never having a bath, and expect to come up smelling of roses, can you? No, this was a smell so foul and strong, it could make your eyes melt.

While Matt and Sienna pulled Alex and Mia out of the ice and away from this mysterious and very smelly frozen entity, the monster saw itself for the first time in its life. Reflected in the ice, the creature saw a swollen mass of scaly skin from which a large twisted beak sprouted between two bulging eyes, and on either side of its body draped two ragged and featherless wings. Being trapped at the bottom of the sea for hundreds of years clearly hadn't done it any favours looks-wise either.

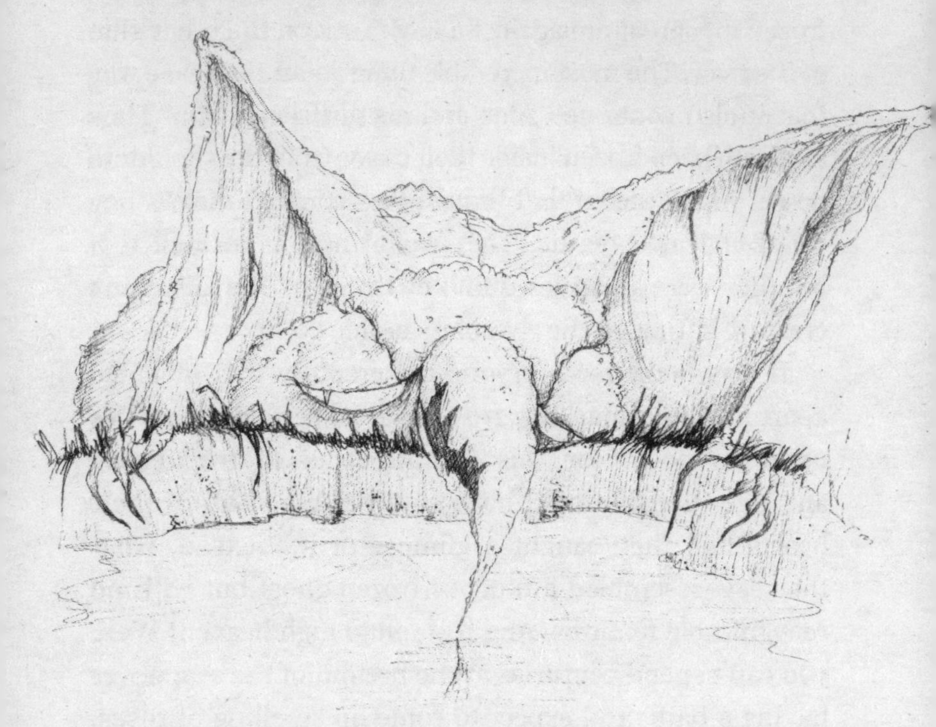

'WHY I AM SO UGLY?'

This is what the monster said, although its beak was such a broken mess that its words sounded more like the effects of violent indigestion than anything else. The monster let out a blood-curdling wail and a torrent of hailstones came from its mouth, sending both couples flying in all directions.

The monster choked and snorted the remaining hailstones out of its beak as Matt, Sienna, Alex and Mia scrambled up the opposite bank and away into the trees.

The monster watched the humans running away. It panted and drooled, the drool turning to icicles that tinkled as they broke off. There before it stretched the ice, reflecting the sun like a blanket of jewels. The grass covered in leaves and flowers on the opposite riverbank so pretty and delicate. The bare branches of the trees swaying gracefully in the breeze. Everywhere the monster looked, it saw beauty, and it felt it did not belong. Like Hoot, it was born of pride, so it wasn't very clever, but it knew it was ugly, and its envy for the beauty it saw all around exploded into uncontrollable rage. The air around the monster froze and swirled into a little storm cloud. It shivered and smashed the river ice with its beak like a headbanger at a rock concert until the river flowed once more.

You may wonder, why all the snow and ice? It's a good question, and one I can answer with a story about a bag of sausages. I recently left a bag of sausages in a warm cupboard by mistake. Stupid thing to do, I know, but then again, I am a forgetful person. Anyway, after a month there was a bad smell and I thought there was a problem with the plumbing or that a mouse had died underneath the cupboard. When at last I found the bag of sausages, they were no longer sausages – they were pure evil. I mean, they had transformed into something truly rotten. The colour of the sausages, the shape, the size, the texture and certainly the smell were completely different from the sausages I had bought, and if *this* is what happens to a bag of sausages after a month in a cupboard, just imagine what happens to a fantastical monster that has been trapped at the bottom of the sea for over three centuries inside a bell and the first experience it has of the modern world is the aching cold of an industrial freezer! Given how ugly and smelly this monster is, I think we're all very lucky it didn't produce something much worse than snow and ice. Anyway, I hope that clears things up, because the monster is about to scream again.

'BUZZARD!'

Somewhere deep inside its body, the creature felt a pulling sensation. It was the same kind of feeling a homing pigeon experiences as it begins its journey home. It's like a form of hunger, but instead of being satisfied by food, the hunger will only be satisfied once the destination has been reached. And home for this monster was the place Buzzard's soul had left his body.

'BUZZ-AAAAAAARD!' wailed the monster, and it flew across the gulping ice flow, smashing its way through the surrounding woods on the other side, splintering trees as if they were mere twigs, and sending both couples diving to the ground.

You will be relieved to know that despite some nasty cuts, bruises, and some serious frostbite in the case of Matt's fingers, both couples survived their encounter with the creature (though the same cannot be said for their relationships, as Mia and Sienna dumped their boyfriends the very next day).

THE CALL OF THE FRUIT BAT

It was only four and half hours since the first news report about Uncle Pogo and Doody had aired, and now every TV station, every radio station and every social media platform was buzzing with sightings and reports of the same storm cloud tearing its way through France. Nobody could see the monster within the cloud or hear its cry as it shot through the sky; they could see only the devastation it left in its wake. Matt's GoPro camera had recorded the entire incident at the frozen river, and most of the planet had seen the clip by now (including his embarrassing argument with Sienna). One of the clearest video clips had been taken by the owner of a French campsite who had filmed the storm cloud smashing through his canteen area like a wrecking ball, before flying away again into the air in a great rainbow-sized arc. While the world tried to work out what this cloud-thing was, the monster inside the cloud had already injured hundreds of people, flattened an entire cathedral, frozen rivers and streams, crushed woodlands, destroyed two motorway bridges and a French service station, which to be honest was never that nice anyway, especially the toilets.

It must be an alien! It must be the effects of global warming! It must be an act of war! An act of terrorism! A publicity stunt for a new action movie! No, no, no!

A riot of rumours and speculation had been unleashed online, and even the most laid-back and sensible people turned into terrified idiots. There were so many different theories flying around, they drowned out the opinions of the few individuals who had correctly worked out that all of this must have something to do with Doody and Pogo's haul from the Greek shipwreck. And even they didn't have the answer the two main questions:

1. What is it?
2. How can it be stopped from smashing everything in its path to pieces?

The only thing everyone could agree on was the direction it was travelling; it was generally heading north, and it was doing so at a staggering speed.

Nelson was glued to the news on the TV screen in his parents' bedroom, safe in the knowledge that they wouldn't catch him because his mother was also glued to the TV in the living room and, having spoken with the doctors tending Doody and Pogo, his father was cooking something in the kitchen that sizzled loudly and smelt of onions and sherry.

Nelson grabbed the remote control and switched off

the TV. He had just heard a noise, like someone knocking on a door in another room upstairs. He held his breath and sat very still, hoping he wasn't about to get caught by his parents. Cold air was creeping under the door and chilling his toes. Had his parents left the front door open?

Nelson slowly rose to his feet and peered around the bedroom door. He could hear his parents talking downstairs over a mix of TV and cooking sounds. Across the landing he could see his own bedroom door was still closed, but there were sounds of someone or something moving around behind the door. There was the tinkling of broken glass. The fluttering of loose paper. The unmistakeable metallic clang of his tin of pencils being knocked over.

Had someone just broken into the house? Should he call down to his parents?

Nelson crossed the landing and listened at his door. The draft coming from beneath it suggested his window had somehow opened. He threw open the door and saw something that shocked him more than if he had been slapped by a nun.

A dozen fruit bats were hanging all around his bedroom, from the bookshelves, curtain rail, window frame and from the ceiling lamp hung four fruit bats like a living umbrella, all with their quivering outstretched wings touching and their mouths open wide.

Nelson could not speak or move or think. He just stood there with one hand on the door handle and his jaw hanging open while a cool wind blew in through his broken window.

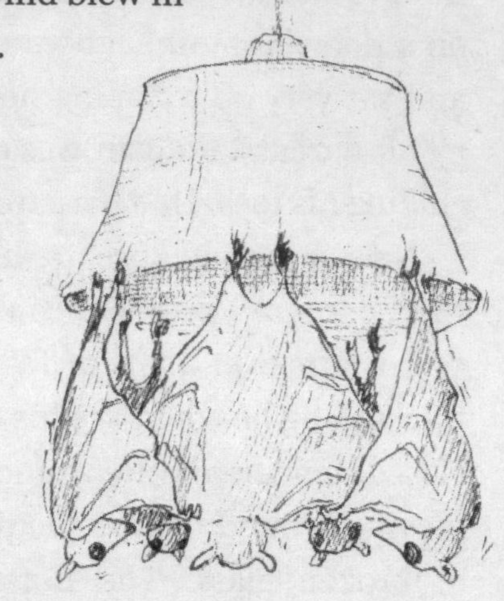

'Master Nelson? Can you hear me?'

It was Miser, but he wasn't in the room. His voice seemed to be coming out of the air.

'Miser?' whispered Nelson breathlessly.

'Ah! There you are!' said Miser, but still Nelson looked around, baffled.

'Wh-what's going on? Where are you?'

'You must stand in the middle of the fruit bats for a better reception, Master Nelson. I can barely hear you.'

Nelson slowly closed the door behind him and did as instructed. There was something deeply unsettling about having so many bats hanging in your bedroom, and it didn't help that they all kept their mouths wide open so that their tiny teeth were on display.

Unlike his monsters, who had the ability to understand animals, Nelson had no idea what the bats were saying, which is just as well, as they were all having a good laugh at how freaked out Nelson looked from upside down. Here's a taster of what they were saying . . .

Look at this kid. He's totally freaked out.
You'd think he'd never seen a bat before.
Do you reckon he has any snacks?
I could murder a banana right now.
You only just ate before we came out!
So? It's not my fault if I'm hungry again.
Shh! The sooner we get this done,
the sooner we can go back to the zoo and eat.
All right! All right! Keep your fur on!

Without taking his eyes of the chattering bats, Nelson stepped beneath the four hanging from his ceiling lamp, and as he did so, he heard a ringing in his ears. It was like the high-pitched noise you might have experienced after a fireworks display or rock concert. He instinctively flexed his jaw as if this might release the pressure behind his ears and stop them ringing, but it did no good at all.

'What is going on?' Nelson heard his words echo around him as if he were in a cave rather than surrounded by plastic toys and IKEA furniture, and when Miser answered, his voice was as clear as if he were talking straight into both of Nelson's ears at the same time.

'Allow me to explain what is happening, Master Nelson. You have forbidden us from pestering you until your troubles at school are corrected – and quite rightly,

I might add. But I'm afraid something quite terrible has happened, so I sought a different means of communication that I hope will not have been too invasive.'

'Invasive? Miser, my windows are smashed in! There are bats in my bedroom! They're all over the place just staring at me! In fact, it looks like they are laughing at me!'

'I assure you, they are not laughing at you, Master Nelson. They are here to help us.'

'Help us? What's going on? Where are you?'

'As usual, we are here in London Zoo. Or to be more precise, I am standing in the Fruit Bat Forest in an identical configuration to yours. The high-pitch noise you hear is being made by the bats. You will notice their mouths are wide open. This is because they are emitting an extremely high-frequency sound that travels for many miles and our voices are being carried on that very same frequency.'

A moment passed while Nelson stared at the quivering

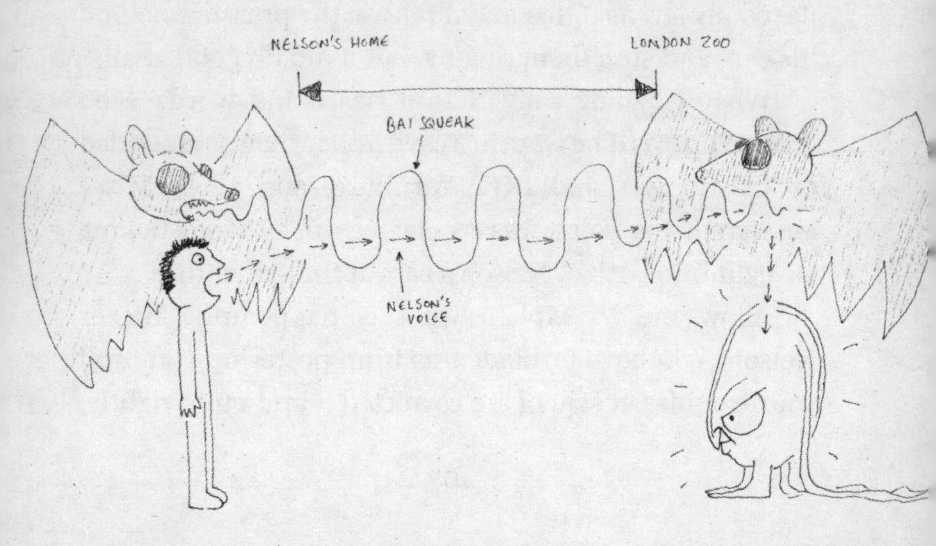

fruit bats. Only now did he notice they were not placed randomly around his room but rather like little satellite dishes, positioned to bounce sound in and out of the window.

'Master Nelson? Are you still there?'

'Uhh . . . yes. Yes, I'm here.'

'We understand you did not do as we suggested and contact your uncle Pogo.'

'No I didn't. I'm really sorry.'

'And now the monster has escaped.'

'All right, don't go on about it.'

'A tremendous mistake.'

'Look, I feel bad about it, OK? But what am I supposed to do?'

'I'm afraid none of us knows what to do.'

'Wow. I'm so glad we had this conversation.'

'We thought you might have ideas or had perhaps learned of some information from the news.'

'I only know some stuff about it from Doody and Pogo's TV show the other night.'

'Anything at all could be useful, Master Nelson.'

'OK, well, it was made the same way you lot were, you know, the sin extractor. But this monster, it ate the other six before they grew to full size.'

'Did you say it *ate them*?'

'Yeah, I know – it's disgusting, isn't it?'

'On the contrary, I think we can safely assume this monster must be born of greed.'

'Right, except it can fly, and Hoot's the only one who can do that.'

'Do you think it could be born of pride?'

'It could be. I saw a painting of the man it was extracted from. He was a podgy man and his name was . . . Buzzard. Yeah that was it. Buzzard. I can't remember his first name. Anyway, he died at St Paul's Cathedral right after his monsters were made. Fell to his death on the cathedral floor.'

'Then this is where the monster will go.'

'To St Paul's?'

'The point on earth where this Buzzard fellow died will hold the last residue of his soul. The monster will be drawn to this fragment of Buzzard's soul just as we are drawn to yours.'

'Right. And what will it do when it gets there?'

'Ahh . . .'

'What do you mean, "Ahh"?'

'I mean to say, finding a tiny trace of Buzzard's soul will do nothing to quench its grief, which must be immense, and so the creature will then very likely, if I may borrow a phrase you are fond of, *go absolutely bananas*.'

Nelson could already imagine what 'going bananas' would look like: St Paul's Cathedral being smashed like all those French villages on the TV news.

'Nelson? Have you left the windows open?' It was Nelson's mother. She was already at the top of the stairs. He could hear the floorboards creak as she crossed the landing.

'It's my mum! How am I supposed to explain all this to her?'

It was too late to answer that question. Nelson's mother opened the door, and the bats took to the air like a bunch of gloves in a tornado.

'OH MY GOD!' she cried, and Nelson dropped to the floor, covering his head with his hands.

'BATS!' she screamed as she swatted at them with one arm while the other covered her face. 'STEPHEN!' she cried.

'JUST COMING!' was his father's reply from downstairs.

Nelson crawled under his bed as the bats rushed to get out of the broken windows.

'WHAT THE HECK IS GOING ON?' shouted Nelson's father as he ran up the stairs, but by the time he had arrived at Nelson's bedroom door, all the bats had gone. (And you will be pleased to hear, they all returned to the zoo. Except one. There's always one. She's out there somewhere having a whale of a time.)

'There were bats, Stephen! Bats everywhere! Look! They smashed the window! Nelson? Nelson, where are you?'

'I'm under the bed!'

Nelson's mother and father dropped to their knees and peered under the bed.

'Are you OK, love? Did they bite you?'

'Uh . . . no. No I'm fine, thanks.'

'What on earth happened, Nelse?' said Nelson's father.

'Load of bats, Dad,' said Nelson. 'Just flew in through the window. I dunno why.'

'First Pogo and Doody, then this storm-cloud thing smashing up France, and now bats in the bedroom? Blimey! It's like the world is coming to an end, son.'

Nelson's father had no idea just how right he was.

On the other side of London, in the Fruit Bat Forest of London Zoo, Miser stepped out from the ring of bats hanging above his head and addressed his six fellow monsters, all waiting eagerly for news.

'I have learned some very useful facts about this monster, but sadly our call was cut short by the arrival Nelson's mother.'

'Oh, not his mum,' groaned Spike. 'We just got him in more trouble. And that means he's gonna hate us even more now.'

'That may well be so.' Miser turned to one fruit bat in particular and nodded respectfully before addressing him. 'Thank you, Godfrey. I do not know if this will come to anything, but you and your fellow fruit bats have been most helpful tonight.'

'We are happy to help if it means stopping this monster,' said Godfrey. 'Let's hope your human friend is willing to help too.'

*

Nelson was supposed to be revising for a maths test, but

now he was making up his bed in the spare room while his parents tidied up the broken glass and mess the bats had made in his bedroom. How on earth was he supposed to revise, let alone sleep, after what just happened? A stupid grief-riddled monster was on its way to destroy London. Should he warn his parents? Run into the street and tell everyone to take cover? Of course he couldn't do that. No one would believe him.

'I've got to do something,' said Nelson to himself, but it was difficult to get his thoughts together as they were still jumbled by the bat experience. He needed to pin the facts down in order to make sense of them, and among his homework Nelson found the two things everyone needs in a confusing situation: a pen (or a pencil; you can't be choosy in an emergency) and some paper.

It didn't matter that this piece of paper already had a half-written book report on it. Nelson used the space below to write down everything he was thinking.

Doody and Pogo in hospital – MY FAULT!!
Now big invisible monster on its way
to destroy London – NIGHTMARE!!
Maths test tomorrow – NIGHTMARE!!

Nelson imagined Celeste reading the list over his shoulder and he felt ashamed for including his own problems at school when the lives of thousands, maybe even millions of other people were at stake. And what would the monster do after it had destroyed London? Would it just keep going until the world had been destroyed?

There *was* something he could do. He could gather up his own monsters and he could try to stop this monster. At least he knew exactly where it was headed, and surely seven against one was a good bet? But then again, tomorrow was Monday, he had a test in the morning, and if he failed he would be in a world of trouble. Nelson grabbed the pen again and furiously crossed the last line out.

~~Maths test tomorrow – NIGHTMARE!!~~

Beneath this Nelson wrote . . .

Revise for test
Save the world

He knew he could choose only one of these options. And Nelson chose to save the world.

WHAT TO PACK WHEN YOU ARE OFF TO SAVE THE WORLD

The broken glass had been cleared and cardboard from cereal packets stuck over Nelson's broken windows to keep out the wind, but it was still too cold for him to sleep in there.

Nelson's mum and dad peered around the spare bedroom door, and light from the landing illuminated his sleeping face.

'Goodnight, Nelse. Sleep tight,' whispered his dad, pulling the door shut.

His performance of 'boy fast asleep' was worthy of an award, but there would be no sleep for Nelson tonight. He opened his eyes and threw back his duvet to reveal that he was already dressed in his black hooded sweater, dark blue jeans and grey-and-white sneakers. From the cupboard, he took out the backpack already filled with everything he usually took on his nights out with his monsters.

- ✔ **One empty water bottle.** Nelson planned to fill it up later, but with something far more refreshing than ordinary tap water.
- ✔ **One packet of sticking plasters** for small cuts and grazes. These happened to be decorated with images of characters from *SpongeBob SquarePants.*
- ✔ **Three packets of chewing gum.** His monsters loved this stuff, and a mouthful of gum was guaranteed to keep them all quiet for a few minutes.
- ✔ **Matches.** He had never used the matches, but they always seemed like a good thing to pack.
- ✔ **Gloves.** Even on summer nights, Nelson's hands always got cold after midnight.
- ✔ **Mexican wrestler mask.** Just in case he needed to hide his appearance from people or surveillance cameras.
- ✔ **Oyster card.** You never know when you might need to jump on a train or a bus.
- ✔ **Two extra-large Fruit & Nut chocolate bars.** Snacks are important.
- ✔ **Pen and paper.** Always more useful than you would think!
- ✔ **Mobile phone and charger.** Useful for Google Maps and watching YouTube clips of skateboarders falling over (Stan's favourite thing in the world).

- ✔ **Portable Bluetooth speaker.** Music was fun to listen to, and also had surprising effects on Hoot.
- ✔ **A satsuma.** Along with clementines, the best travelling fruit there is. Bananas always get smooshed, apples bruised, and plums – just forget it. The satsuma or the clementine is the go-to fruit for all sensible heroes. Small and already wrapped by nature.
- ✔ **Face flannel and soap.** After a night out on an adventure, it was important to wash away the dirt before you walked back into your house. Also great for dealing with sticky hands after eating the previously mentioned satsuma.
- ✔ **Head torch.** This was very useful for getting around at night-time and leaving your hands free for the last thing on the list, which was also the only thing Nelson *hadn't* packed in his backpack . . .
- ✔ **Electric scooter** that his uncle Pogo had custom-made for him (it looked like a regular stand-up scooter, but it had a top speed of forty-five miles per hour). It was waiting for him under a plastic sheet against the side passage of the house. He would have to be very careful to sneak it through the gate without alerting his parents.

As Nelson pulled the backpack over his shoulder, the words 'I'M A WINNER' caught his eye. It was the slogan on the T-shirt of the fluffy rhino.

Though Ivan had meant it as a good-luck charm for his exams, Nelson felt a desire to trade that luck for the task ahead, and so he shoved the fluffy rhino into the top of his backpack.

It had been several weeks since he last snuck out of the house, but on all of those previous occasions, it had been to have fun with his seven monster friends. This time he had no idea if he would make it home alive.

FRIENDS REUNITED

Crush was the first to sense it and he started running towards the outer fence before he even knew what he was doing. 'Honk! Honk! Honk! Honk! Hoooooooonk!'

''E's comin'!' shouted Stan, who had joined Crush, Spike, Miser and Nosh bounding along the pathway towards the giant aviary. They all felt the same joyous feeling: Nelson was coming! The monsters cheered and jumped as they ran through the zoo. The animals picked up on the happy vibrations resonating from the monsters and began to think nice things, like being reunited with lost family members or returning to their jungles, oceans, forests, deserts or, in the case of the dung beetles, piles of fresh dung.

The iron fence at the rear of the zoo backed directly on to Regent's Canal, and the monsters pressed their faces between the bars and strained to be the first to catch a glimpse of Nelson.

'Is he . . . is he here?' panted Puff as he joined the others at the fence.

'I can't see 'im yet! But 'e ain't far! I can feel it!' said Stan, breathless with excitement.

All the monsters fell silent and stared at the footpath. They knew he was going to appear any second now as certainly as they knew it was night-time.

'Ta-daaaaah!' sang Hoot, and the monsters looked up to see the great golden bird descending from the night sky with Nelson hanging from his claws. His monsters cheered and as soon as Nelson had dropped the scooter and his feet had touched the ground, they were all over him. Crush leaped into his arms, and Nosh was hugging him before Nelson could even speak. Stan couldn't stop laughing and slapping Nelson on the back while Spike began to cry with happiness.

'Quite an entrance, wouldn't you say? Well, I certainly would. You see, I knew Master Nelson was on his way, and so what did I do? I swooped down, or rather I *soared majestically* like this, you see . . .' Hoot continued to describe how he had picked Nelson up from the pathway beside the canal as if it were a greater achievement than climbing Mount Everest, but no one was listening.

'So what do we do now?' said Stan in the most hopeful and eager tone of voice anyone had ever heard from him.

'Well, I think we should try to save the world,' said Nelson, and the monsters cheered. Well, not all the monsters cheered. Puff was in the midst of yawning, and Hoot was still talking to himself.

'Spike, we're really gonna need some of your snot tonight.'

Yes, you heard correctly. Nelson has just asked for some of Spike's snot. Now, don't go getting all squeamish. Spike is a walking, talking cactus, so instead of blowing mucus out of his nostrils like you and I would, Spike produces a thick green gel similar to aloe vera. Unlike snot, aloe vera is packed with extremely high levels of goodness. It's the opposite of disgusting – it's fantastic!

'Go on then. Let's get this over with,' moaned Spike.

Nelson took out his water bottle, unscrewed the cap and began to tickle the spot just beneath Spike's nostrils.

'Ahhh-tchoo!' sneezed Spike, and jets of thick green gel shot out of his nose.

Nelson caught it in his water bottle and continued to

tickle Spike and make him sneeze until he had filled it right to the top. And then he took a big gulp for himself. (Even though I told you Nelson was not collecting snot but a very healthy plant extract, you are still finding this disgusting, aren't you?)

The effect was instant. The green liquid dissolved and dispersed through Nelson's body, wiping out all of the toxins that had built up from consuming modern foods and drinks and breathing city air. It left his entire body and mind as clear and refreshed as a mountain stream. Nelson's thoughts, which until now had been jumbled, suddenly lined up like soldiers on parade; his muscles twanged, eager to move; his lungs and airways were clear of dust particles; his eyesight was twice as sharp, and his hearing twice as clear. This is how members of tribes living natural lives feel all of the time, but for folks living in the modern world, this feeling is rare. Spike's green liquid also happened to taste a bit lemony, which was a nice bonus.

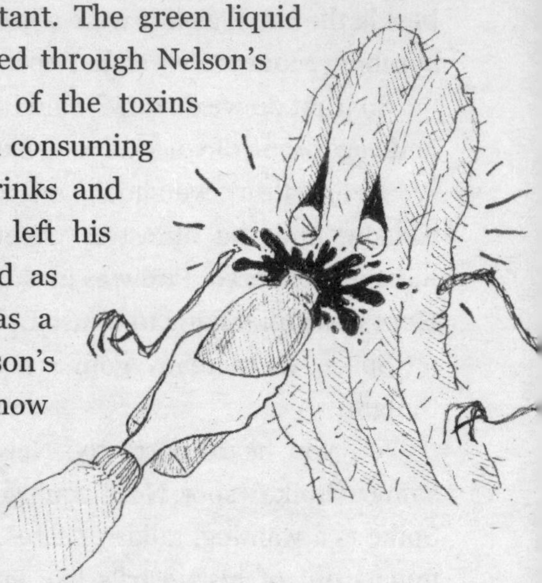

It was Nosh who had discovered the power of Spike's snot. He had been drawn to a handkerchief covered in green liquid and only after licking the thing clean had he discovered it had been used by Spike to catch a sneeze. Nosh had felt the rush of his body being cleansed and supercharged and didn't waste a second in sharing his discovery with the others. Bites, stings and burns they had incurred over the summer had all been cured instantly by this green liquid, and just one sip made them feel like they'd just received an upgrade.

As the other monsters took their sip from the water bottle, Nelson began to spell out the plan he'd been thinking of on the way over.

'We know this monster is heading to St Paul's, so we can be there before it arrives, and when it does . . . well, I think we should set up an ambush and trap it somehow.'

'LET'S KILL IT!' roared Stan, and the others cheered, their spirits higher than they'd been in weeks.

'You can't kill it. It's a monster like you, and you lot are immortal, right?'

The monsters didn't answer. Instead they fell silent and looked at the ground as if embarrassed to answer.

'What?' said Nelson. 'Why have you gone all quiet?'

Puff cleared his throat, rolled on to his back and stretched his paws into the air. He loved the effect of the cactus juice. Other than fear, it was the only thing that woke his sleepy mind and body up.

'Nuffin is immortal, Nelson. Everything comes to an end . . . in the end. And monsters – we can be destroyed, but only in a fire as hot as the sun.'

'Ah-ha!' said Miser, his lips smacking, having taken a sip of cactus juice. 'Puff is on to something!'

'What? What is Puff talking about?' asked Nelson.

'Nosh has got a furnace in his belly that could roast a hundred monsters.'

'YEAH!' roared Nosh! 'LEMME DO DAT! I WANNA EAT DAT FING AND ROAST IT IN MA BELLY!'

The monsters were excited. They bounced around and panted like dogs desperate to go for a walk. Crush's short, sharp honks had the effect of an air horn on a crowd of football supporters. Only Nelson felt uneasy at this plan.

'Whoa, Nosh!' said Nelson. 'It's not just gonna turn up at St Paul's like a takeaway pizza for you to munch, is it? It's a *monster*. A really angry, crazy monster that can fly really fast and freeze a whole forest and kill anything in its way. I mean, it's gonna be nuts just trying to catch this thing, let alone feed it to you.'

Stan grinned and slammed a fist into his other palm. 'Bring it on, baby!'

Nelson looked out across the park and at the city surrounding it. 'Oh man. This city's gonna get wrecked in the process.' He turned to Miser. 'Is there any way we can stop it from coming to London?'

'There is indeed.'

'Really? I was totally expecting you to say no to that.'

''Tis quite simple. We take Buzzard's soul far away from the cathedral and the city to a safer, less populated location. Maybe woodland or a costal area?' Miser's fingers drummed together in front of his nose as his bulbous eyes rolled around in their sockets. Miser was never more creepy-looking than when he was hatching a plan.

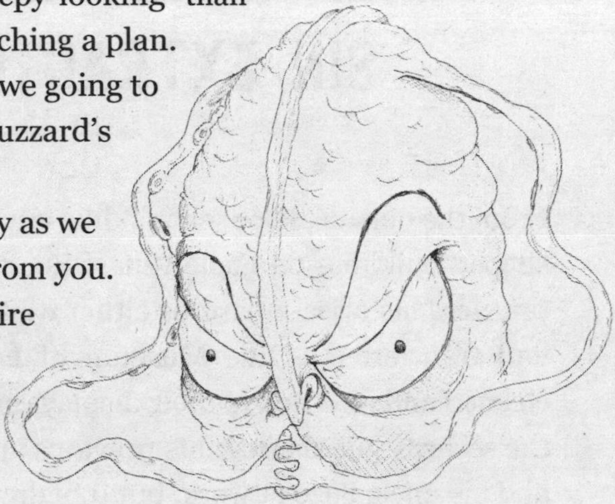

'And how are we going to do that? Catch Buzzard's soul, I mean.'

'Just as simply as we were extracted from you. All we shall require is a needle from the sin extractor and a vessel in which to contain the remains of Buzzard's soul.'

'Oh for cryin' out loud.' Stan was clearly fed up. 'Why can't we just have normal plan, eh? A good old-fashioned punch-up not good enough for you lot though, is it? Nah – too easy. Instead we gotta carry some bloke's soul somewhere – I dunno – flippin' miles away and use it like bait to catch this fing who we then 'ave to feed to fatboy over 'ere.'

'Dat plan sounds wicked!' said Nosh eagerly.

And though Nelson didn't quite share Nosh's enthusiasm, he knew it was the only plan they had.

SURLY KAREN AND THE SIN EXTRACTOR

From the outside, it looked just like any of the other box-shaped buildings on Eagle Wharf Road, but inside were priceless historical treasures either waiting to be studied and transferred to the Museum of London, or to be cleaned and returned to their display cases. Nelson knew the security guards from his previous visits to see Doody and his uncle Pogo at work, but tonight Nelson could see through the window that someone new was on duty.

The guard, whose name was Karen, was watching TV on her phone and picking suspiciously at a curry she had just microwaved in a plastic pot, when Nelson knocked on the glass window of her booth.

'Wh-who are you? Eh? W-what do you want?' she stammered while putting down her dinner and switching off her phone.

'Erm . . . my uncle works here. His name is—'

'There's no one working here tonight. It's Sunday.'

'I know, but my uncle usually works here and he always lets me in.'

'Nah. No public access.'

'Honestly. Perry Goldsmith? His nickname is Pogo.

He works with Doody. I mean, Professor John Doody.'

'Yeah, I know 'em, but they're not here. They were in an accident and we're closed to the public.'

'I know, but . . . I was here visiting them the other day, and I left my homework here. They were helping me with it. I know where it is. It's at the back, in the workshop, and . . . and I'll get detention if I don't hand it in tomorrow.'

Surly Karen sucked her teeth as she looked as Nelson's pleading face. Her curry was getting cold, but then again it couldn't get any worse. It had so far been one of the worst curries she had ever eaten. She clearly had no intention of letting Nelson into the building, which is why Nelson started to cry. His earlier performance of 'boy fast asleep' had been great, but this performance of 'boy very upset' was off the charts!

Between great blubbering gulps and sniffs, Nelson managed to explain how much trouble he would be in at school and at home if he failed to bring in his homework. Surly Karen was mortified. Not only did she find it deeply disturbing to be stuck in front of a weeping child, she couldn't help but find herself remembering what it was like being at school. All that pressure to keep up with the clever kids. The teachers, some of them more boring than watching a beard grow, droning on about things Karen did not fully understand still to this day. Before she knew what she was doing, Karen had raised her hand as if to silence Nelson and grabbed the master set of keys hanging inside a steel box nailed to the wall.

You should have heard Nelson's monsters. They were cheering and applauding him so much that it was extremely difficult for Nelson to keep up the sad act. Crush honked so much that Nelson began to blush.

Seconds later, Nelson, Stan, Miser and Crush were marching between the towering metal shelves stacked with boxes and bags and bottles and vials and cans – all of which contained some kind of historical discovery related to London – from Roman coins to a human skull dating back to the Iron Age. Hoot and Nosh remained outside, while Puff and Spike were positioned close to Karen. She waited by the exit door rather than follow Nelson. She may have been moved enough to let him in, but she did not want to get too close to the boy. It made her deeply uncomfortable to be around so much emotion.

The fluorescent lights flickered on automatically as Nelson made his way to a workshop at the far end. It was a large space and it smelt like a mixture of wood, wet clay and glue. Studio lights on tall stands surrounded the area, though the lights were off now. Doody and Pogo used this area to test and investigate Sir Christopher Wren's inventions and theories for their TV show, the most important of which was lying under a clear plastic sheet in the corner.

'Found it yet?' shouted Karen.

'I think it's here somewhere!' replied Nelson.

Stan whipped off the plastic sheet as impressively as a tiny matador, and all at once the monsters began to twitch and shiver. Like kryptonite to Superman or sunshine to Count Dracula, the sin extractor had a powerfully negative effect on the monsters. It was as if the needles were a monster magnet, pulling them across the floor towards it.

'What's going on?' whispered Nelson as Stan grabbed hold of his leg.

The colour was draining out of Stan as if even colour could not resist the pull of the needles.

'I dunno! Just get it done and cover it up!'

Miser reached out with both of his long tentacles to pipes on opposite walls. Taking a firm grip, he made himself into a living barrier to stop himself and the other monsters from sliding any closer.

'What's going on over there?' shouted Puff, who like

Spike was too far away to feel the magnetic pull of the sin extractor.

There was no time to answer Puff. Nelson leaned over the extractor table. Thousands of tiny metal needles arranged in intricate, swirling patterns pointed up at him.

Nelson gripped one of the needles at the base with his thumb and forefinger and began to wobble it like you would a baby tooth that has outstayed its welcome in your mouth. There was a very gentle *click* and it came away from the table base.

'Hurry up!' groaned Stan, who was clinging to a chair leg and beginning to feel his own horns work loose like teeth being pulled out by a dentist.

As Nelson carefully lifted out the sin-extractor needle, he found that what he was holding was just the tip of a much longer needle. It was at least three times the length, in fact. The middle was twisted like a fine corkscrew, and both ends were equally sharp, though one end – the end that had been beneath the table – was black.

'Got it!' shouted Nelson, and he jabbed the needle deep into the fluffy rhino for safe keeping, stuffed the rhino into his backpack, and flung the plastic sheet back over the sin extractor. At once the powerful vacuuming effect stopped.

Nelson took some paper from his backpack and waved it triumphantly as he approached Karen.

'Thanks so much, Karen. Seriously, you're a lifesaver.'

'S'OK,' said Karen, and she returned to her small room and her terrible curry but with a nice feeling inside for having helped a weeping child.

Outside, Nelson did a quick headcount.

'Everyone here? Miser, Stan, Spike, Nosh, Crush, Puff. Great. We got the needle! Let's go and get Buzzard.'

You may have noticed that Nelson did not mention Hoot. That is because there was no need to be reminded of where Hoot was as he had grown to the size of a house.

BIG HEAD BIRD BRAIN

It had been months ago on a warm summer night when Nelson had discovered how to inflate Hoot.

Nelson and his monsters had been sitting in the uppermost branches of an oak tree in the park watching Hoot perform one of his legendary aerial displays to a piece of classical music ('Dance of the Reed Pipes' by Tchaikovsky on this occasion). The music was played through Nelson's Bluetooth speaker, and when Hoot finally came in to land, they had all burst into applause. It is important to note that none of them had thought Hoot's display any good; in fact, it had to have been one of the most stupid things any of them had ever seen, but it was SO bad that they had actually enjoyed it and rewarded the silly bird for making them laugh so much with a rousing chorus of whistles, cheers and above all, applause. Hoot had no idea their response was sarcastic and had continued to bow to Nelson and the others over and over again. It was after about thirty-five seconds or so that Nelson noticed it. Hoot's head was getting bigger. Much bigger. The more they clapped, the bigger it got, and it wasn't long before Hoot's head had tripled in size.

His body grew just enough to support the giant head, which didn't stop growing until Nelson waved to the rest of the monsters to stop.

'Guys, stop. Stop! Look! Look what's happened to him,' Nelson had said, and the other monsters had burst into hysterics as Hoot gasped in shock at his new appearance.

'Do you feel all right, Hoot? Are you OK?' Nelson was the only one who felt concern, but the least concerned of all was Hoot.

'Good gracious . . . I have become huge! Ha ha! Look at me! I am, dare I say it, even more magnificent than ever before!'

Clearly Hoot had never felt better, and so from that night on, when Nelson and his monsters needed to fly somewhere together, they had only to shower Hoot with applause and he would grow big enough to carry them all through the sky.

Hoot had never enjoyed himself as much as he was enjoying himself right now. His wings the size of a small plane and his palm-leaf-sized golden feathers rippling as he sang along to his favourite song playing through Nelson's Bluetooth speaker, 'The Impossible Dream' (the Andy Williams version was his favourite), Hoot's right claw clasped a rope ladder they had 'borrowed' from the Regent's Park adventure playground, and it was upon this ladder that Nelson and the rest of the monsters hung on tight.

'Gawd, I hate that bird,' snarled Stan through gritted

teeth, his eyes clenched against the wind.

'Shh! Don't let him hear you say that,' said Nelson.

If any of them said anything that might deflate Hoot's ego, he would return to his normal size, and then they would all fall out of the sky. Nosh groaned loudly, not because of Hoot's singing, but because he hadn't eaten for at least ten minutes. Nelson had given him strict instructions to work up a fierce appetite in preparation for eating the monster, but for Nosh, ten minutes without food is like two weeks without food for you and me. Drool ran from the corners of his great big mouth and on to Nelson below him.

'Great singing, Hoot!' cried Nelson as he wiped Nosh's drool from his hood with his sleeve.

'Why, thank you, dear boy!' crowed Hoot, before returning to the song and singing with even more tuneless gusto.

If the others hadn't had to cling to the rope ladder, they would have stuck their fingers in their ears.

Crush's eyes were closed tight and he clung to Nelson's neck, every so often letting out a long, low honking noise that spread warmth through Nelson's chest. Despite this lovely warm feeling, the powerful sense of purpose Nelson had felt earlier at the prospect of being reunited with his monsters to save the world was dwindling with every mile they flew. Turning their idea into reality began to feel a bit stupid at worst, naïve at best. Would they really be able to trap Buzzard's soul and use it as bait to draw the monster

away from London? It was impossible to imagine. What he certainly could imagine was the struggle they would have in capturing the creature and feeding it to Nosh. It would be as far from easy as you can get.

The streets below them were empty. Everyone was too consumed with watching the rampaging abomination in France on their screens to bother going outside. This was just as well, as the sight of a boy flying through the sky on a rope ladder would have probably blown their tiny minds.

*

Meanwhile in France, things had not only gone from bad to worse, they had moved on to absolutely dreadful and were now hurtling towards downright terrifying. Scientists from all around the world were being consulted, but none of them could even agree on what it was they were dealing with, let alone come up with a solution. All airlines were grounded. All trains were cancelled. All boats docked, and all roads cleared. The people of France cowered in their homes watching their screens, hoping their village, town or city wasn't next in line for a punishing visit from whatever it was. No one knew their only hope of salvation had just landed on the roof of St Paul's Cathedral.

BLOOD IN THE CATHEDRAL

Nelson crouched on the roof of St Paul's. The powerful gusts of wind generated by Hoot's great wings blew the hood back off his head and whipped dust into his eyes.

'Hoot!' shouted Nelson. 'You can't land on the roof. You'll need to be smaller again!'

'Oh, just a little longer. I do so love being large! Look at me! Have you ever seen anything more gorgeous in your life? Nooo! You have not!' crowed Hoot, but the stone roof crumbled like chalk beneath Hoot's claws.

'Hoot, please! You can't land while you're that big! You're too heavy! You might break something else or go right through the roof!' Nelson turned to the other six monsters, shrugged and said, 'You know what to do.'

And they did. With great glee, the monsters began to hurl the most appalling insults at Hoot. Even Crush's honks sounded incredibly rude.

You utter wombat!
Your singing is so bad, I was just sick in my own mouth!
You're a massive feather-faced loser!
You're a pus-coloured nitwit!
You're a royal pain in the backside!
You're a fart-breathing bozo from the planet Berk!

And so it went on. These were quite possibly the worst things anyone had said in or around St Paul's Cathedral since Sir Christopher had expressed his frustrations with the ghastly Master Buzzard, but the monsters' insults did at least achieve the intended results: Hoot was back to his original size in no time at all, and the other monsters were feeling much more cheerful again.

'Yes, well . . . I can see you all enjoyed that very much,' said Hoot in a quavering voice that suggested tears might be on the way.

'Hey. Come on, Hoot. We only said that stuff to bring you down to size,' said Nelson. The other monsters, especially Stan, Spike and Puff, looked as if they were about to hurl a few more insults, but Nelson beat them to it by saying, 'We didn't really mean it, and, look, we wouldn't be here on the top of St Paul's if it wasn't for you.'

This one compliment (plus a few chunks of Fruit & Nut) was all it took for Hoot's chest to inflate and his eyes to sparkle again. Nelson turned around to face the others.

'Right, everyone look around. We need to find a way in.'

BANG! Stan was standing on the other side of the roof and had just punched a fire-escape door right off its hinges.

'Found a way!' shouted Stan.

'Stan! Please! Don't just start smashing the place up! We have to be quiet and careful or they'll have the police around here,' pleaded Nelson in a strangled whisper.

'You wanted a way in, so there's ya way in! Unless you don't want my 'elp?'

'I do, I do, but please just ask me before you smash any more doors to bits, OK?' Nelson took out his Mexican wrestler mask from his backpack and pulled it over his head. There were bound to be lots of CCTV cameras inside and though he could not avoid them, he could at least hide his identity from them.

Bits of wood from the smashed fire-escape door covered two flights of very narrow stairs that led directly down to another door, this one metal and painted black. Together, Nelson and his monsters leaned against the metal door at the base of the stairs until the hinges split and the door fell with a loud CLANG! on to the floor of a corridor.

Nelson peered into the corridor while holding his monsters back with one hand. If there were security guards around, they must have heard the noise. The CLANG echoed long after the door had fallen. They would have to move very quickly from here on.

'Whispering Gallery this way,' whispered Nelson, and he ran to the right, staying close enough to the wall that his jacket made a whizzing sound as it rubbed against the stone. Nelson's monsters weren't just keeping up with him; they seemed to be fighting over who got to run behind him, which meant there was way too much tripping and snarling and pushing and shoving.

'Down here, and stop fighting,' whispered Nelson, pointing to a very wide, open stone staircase cordoned off by a red rope between brass barriers. Over the rope went Nelson, but the rush to be first behind him meant the monsters became tangled in the rope and brought the brass barriers clanging to the ground.

Before Nelson had time to tell them off, a light came on at the foot of the stairwell.

'Who's up there?' said a man's voice from below.

Whoever it was, Nelson could hear, from their footsteps and jangling keys, that they were already climbing the stairs quickly.

Nelson silently mouthed the words, '*Look out!*' and he ran to the other side of the corridor to hide behind a wide stone pillar with Crush clinging to his neck. The other monsters did not need to hide but instead backed away from the staircase without taking their eyes off it. A tall man in his late fifties appeared and instantly reminded Nelson of a badger. His hair was black with grey-and-white streaks and he was dressed in a black-and-white security uniform. In his hand was an unlit torch that he held like a weapon.

'Who's there?' he shouted, and when no one answered, he shone his torch into the dark parts of the corridor.

Nelson didn't realize his backpack was peeking out from behind the pillar. He just stood there, thinking he was well hidden.

'Dear boy! A man is coming towards you!' cried Hoot, and Crush began to honk nervously.

Nelson couldn't say anything; he just had to close his eyes and hope his monsters could do something in time.

'Hold your breath,' said Puff, and a fart as loud and as long as the noise of a passing motorbike filled the air.

The security guard's knees buckled, his eyes rolled back in their sockets, and along with his torch, he fell towards the ground. He would have sustained one heck of a nose bleed had Puff not dived between him and the stone floor. Instead, the security guard landed comfortably and rolled gently on to the floor, sound asleep.

'That was close,' said Nelson, peering out from behind the pillar but still covering his mouth.

They moved away from the purple gas still filling the air and ran down the stairs as originally intended. Though the monsters could not be heard by anyone else, Nelson had to keep shushing them like naughty toddlers in order to listen out for more guards. Ironically, the monsters were making a terrible din as they all made their way to the Whispering Gallery. It may have been due to the fact they'd been spending so much time apart from Nelson lately, but all of the monsters had wanted to be as close to Nelson as possible. Crush honked and honked until Nelson relented and carried him in his arms again. This had been a bad decision, for it only made the other monsters more jealous.

'That's it! That's enough! It doesn't matter which one of you is behind me! We're supposed to be finding the spot where Buzzard died, and you're all acting like a bunch of spoilt kids!'

The monsters fell silent under Nelson's glare. Taking a breath, Nelson turned around and looked down at the floor of the cathedral.

'Well . . . I remember that way leads to Christopher Wren's library and laboratory,' said Nelson, pointing to a lower balcony on the opposite side to them. 'So I s'pose when Buzzard fell, it must have been on that side.'

What a long way to fall. The thought made Nelson shudder, but there was no time to dwell on gruesome thoughts or anything else for that matter. Seven of the doors surrounding the gallery had just opened, and through each one a security guard appeared.

'There! Over there! I see him!' said one of the guards, and they all began running towards Nelson.

'Oh no,' said Nelson.

Puff and Nosh ran one way, Spike and Stan the other in order to block the guards. The guards began shouting and freaking out at the invisible monster barrier they had just been blocked by.

'Hoot! Hold on to me and fly me down!' said Nelson as he swung a leg over the balcony and lifted himself up so that he was sitting facing the biggest fall of his life.

'Right you are!' said Hoot.

But no sooner had he opened his wings for take-off, he was sent tumbling sideways by a door flung open by another guard behind him. The man was very short, but he lunged forwards with astonishing speed, and his hands gripped Nelson's arm above the elbow. Nelson let out a cry, and Crush let out a great blasting 'HOOOOONK!'

Miser wrapped his tentacles around the short guard's body and squeezed. The guard let out a gasp, and Nelson pulled his arm away. But he pulled too hard.

'AAAAH!' screamed Nelson as he toppled from the balcony and fell through the air.

'I say, why is Nelson going without me?' said Hoot, who clearly hadn't understood the mistake.

It all happened so fast, Nelson didn't even have time to close his eyes. The floor of the cathedral seemed to swell beneath him as if it was going to swallow him up, and then . . . it didn't. Nelson felt a great pull from the straps of his backpack, like a seat belt in a fast-braking car, and instead of smashing into the ground, Nelson just swooped, with his face only a few centimetres from the tiles.

Crush fell from Nelson's neck and went rolling across the floor, knocking wooden chairs into the air. Nelson threw his arms in front of his face as his body landed and skidded across the tiles. His chin scraped against the floor and he bit his tongue, but none of it hurt in that moment.

Once his body had stopped sliding, Nelson gasped,

lifted his head and took in what had happened. Despite being terrifyingly late to the rescue, Hoot had caught him, or rather he had caught Nelson's backpack, the contents of which were scattered all over the cathedral floor.

'No need to thank me, dear boy. Hoot is always happy to help, although that was rather unexpected. A little warning next time wouldn't go amiss.'

Breathless and shaken, Nelson pushed himself up on to his knees and threw his head back to see what was going on above.

A cloud of Puff's purple fart gas swirled in the dome of the cathedral. The security men were spluttering and coughing and falling to the ground. He could hear his monsters shouting and hoped that neither they nor the men they were trying to evade had been hurt in the scuffle.

Nelson sneezed and felt blood trickle out of his nose. He hadn't yet realized blood was also dripping from his grazed chin and oozing out of the corner of his mouth, courtesy of his bitten tongue.

'HO-oo-ooo-NK!' Crush was waddling back towards Nelson. His eyes were crossed and he could barely walk in a straight line.

Though he had just survived a great fall, Nelson couldn't help feeling the entire episode had been a disaster. More guards were sure to arrive soon. Police too. There was only so much sleeping gas Puff could produce before Nelson was caught and thrown into the back of a police van. So much for saving the world.

'I say, is that supposed to happen?' Hoot had stopped preening his feathers to point at something on the floor.

Even if Nelson had not been too shaken and breathless to speak, he would still have been rendered speechless by what Hoot was pointing at.

Among the contents of his backpack that had spilt out as he fell from the Whispering Gallery was the little cuddly rhino Ivan had given him. And what made the sight of this rhino truly peculiar was that it was moving.

The movement was slow but deliberate, as if someone had attached an invisible thread to the top of the rhino's head and they were pulling it on its back across the floor. As the rhino slid past the satsuma and broken chocolate bars and matches and water bottle and Oyster card and chewing gum, it gathered speed. Faster and faster it moved, until it went whizzing right past Hoot, reminding Nelson of Ravi zooming along the rugby pitch past the referee.

'HONK!' Crush waddled after it until the rhino suddenly stopped and flipped upside down, its head on the ground, feet in the air, and its whole body quivering as if it were receiving a continuous electric shock.

'Honk! Honk! Honk!' said Crush, which was clearly his way of saying, 'What the heck is going on with this rhino?'

'We comin' down, Nelly-son!' cried Nosh, but Nelson didn't look up to see them leaving the sleeping guards in the Whispering Gallery.

Nelson shuffled on his knees towards the rhino, slowing as he got closer and stopping to crouch beside Crush. He could taste the blood in his mouth now, but it didn't bother him in the slightest. He was transfixed by the quivering upside-down rhino.

'Is it one of those walking-talking toys?' asked Hoot, who had also stepped closer.

But Nelson didn't answer. He looked up again. 'This must be where he fell. It's where Buzzard died. And the extractor needle . . . I stuck it in the rhino for safe keeping.' Nelson needed to think out loud, for what was happening was too great to contain in his brain.

Flop. The rhino had stopped quivering, fallen on to its back and was once again just a toy. Nelson reached out, but even before his fingers touched the fur, he could feel warmth coming from the rhino.

There was a clattering of feet and hooves. His monsters had found their way downstairs.

'Look what we just caught,' said Nelson, lifting up the toy rhino and showing it to the approaching monsters.

'What? It's a toy rhino,' said Stan.

'No,' said Nelson with a triumphant grin. 'It's Buzzard.'

PARIS SMASH

The top of the Eiffel Tower was leaning to one side, and one of its elevators dangled over the River Seine like a discarded yo-yo. The Arc de Triomphe was no longer an arc but a pile of rubble. The surrounding buildings on the Champs-Élysées were covered in a carpet of frost, and an icy wind howled through the empty streets. Not since those dreadful Nazis had strutted in and taken over the city during the Second World War had Paris been in such a terrible way.

Behind windows lurked terrified locals and a few daring folk filming the storm cloud with their smartphones. The monster within the cloud was not interested in landmarks or their historical value; it didn't even know that it was in Paris. It only knew that stopping every now and then to smash things up, especially fancy or beautiful things, temporarily released some of the pain and fury it was feeling.

Gleaming irresistibly in the night like a precious jewel was the golden dome of Les Invalides (pronounced *Lays On-va-leed*), and the monster wanted nothing more than to smash it to bits like you and I might delight in smashing open our boiled egg with a teaspoon. It started its attack by blasting itself into the side of the building like a wrecking ball. Instantly the supporting columns crumbled, and the power providing the exterior lighting was cut, plunging the dome into darkness. This made the monster even more furious. It leaped on top of the dome and began beating it with its rotten wings. The monster may have only been the size of a cow, but its fury was immeasurable.

It pounded the dome so violently that great chunks of stone fell from inside the roof and cracked open the great tomb of Napoleon below.

And just as suddenly it all stopped.

Silence fell.

The monster had stopped smashing the dome and was now sat on the ground beside it, twitching slightly, but otherwise barely moving. Its frosted beak was closed, but its eyes were wide, staring in all directions without blinking as if in a trance. It didn't feel like smashing things any more. Instead it felt something quite different . . .

'Buzzard,' whispered the monster, stretching out one of its wings to point north.

‘Buzzard,’ growled the monster, as if agreeing with itself.

‘Buzzard, Buzzard, Buzzard.’ The monster felt something it had not felt for over 350 years: the soul from which it had been extracted had returned.

THE HAUNTED RHINO

'Do you think it already knows? The monster, I mean. Do you think it knows Buzzard's soul is back in the world?' Nelson had just reached the top of the stairs to the roof of St Paul's and was so puffed that he had to kneel on the ground to get his breath back.

'Course it does,' wheezed Spike as he flopped down next to Nelson. 'It's gonna feel it right away, all the way down to its bones. That feeling, that connection we have with you, it's the only thing that makes life worth living.'

'Well then . . . we better get a move on. We don't want that thing coming to London. We gotta get out to the coast where it's wide open and safe.'

'Hello?'

Nelson and his monsters froze. Someone had just called out. Nelson scrambled to his feet. Another guard must have located them on the roof.

'Hello? Is somebody there?' said the voice. But it wasn't coming from inside the cathedral; it was coming from Nelson's backpack. And the backpack moved. 'Hellooo?' said the voice again. Nelson swung the backpack off his shoulders and on to the ground.

Crush jumped up and clung to Nelson's neck. Stan tensed and clenched his fists, and Hoot cocked his head to one side.

'I say, isn't that funny. For a moment there it sounded as if someone was in that bag of yours,' said Hoot.

But there really was something inside the bag.

'Help me. Someone. Please. I fell from a great height and now I'm stuck. Is somebody there who can assist me?' The backpack shook.

Puff hissed like a cornered cat and bared his sharp little teeth.

'HONK!' said Crush, and the backpack seemed to jerk in response.

Stan raised a fist and was about to bring it crashing down on to the backpack when Nelson held up his hand. 'Wait! Just . . . wait a second . . .'

Nelson crouched by his backpack, lifted the top flap and tugged at the drawstring. Crush hugged tightly to Nelson's neck and hid his face as the contents of the backpack spilt on to the floor – among them the chewing gum, the Bluetooth speaker and the fluffy rhino. None of these items were a surprise to Nelson as he had packed them all himself, but there was a surprise when the fluffy rhino stood up and looked at Nelson.

'Is this heaven?' said the rhino, the tip of the-extractor needle just visible at the top of his head.

No one answered. Well, not right away. They were all

speechless, as I'm sure you would be too if a toy rhino started speaking to you.

'Are you an angel?' it said hopefully, and suddenly Nelson understood.

'Buzzard,' said Nelson. 'You're Buzzard, aren't you?'

'Oh yes! Tell me, giant angel boy, have I arrived at the gates of heaven?'

'Umm . . . well . . . no. You're still in London.' Nelson hadn't felt this awkward since he was asked to play Adolf Hitler in a school musical.

'In London? So I am alive? I AM ALIVE! What luck!' cried the little rhino. 'For a moment there, I thought I had fallen to my death! But no! I AM ALIVE! ALIIIIIVE!'

There can be nothing more awkward than having to tell someone they are dead.

'Well, you're kind of alive. I mean, you did die, but that was over three hundred and fifty years ago, and now you've come back as . . . as a cuddly rhino.'

It was only now that Buzzard, understandably, totally freaked out.

'Aaaah!' he cried as he looked down at his fluffy hands, feet and belly.

'Aaaaah!' he cried again when he felt the horn on the end of his nose.

'Aaaaaah!' at the sight of seven monsters staring at him with open mouths.

'Hello there, little fellow! Well, aren't you a noisy thing!' said Hoot, which did not help one bit.

'Aaaaaah!'

'OK, OK, just calm down, Mr Buzzard. Calm down. Everything's gonna be fine. They look strange, but these monsters won't hurt you.'

'Monsters! I AM IN HELL! HELL HATH CLAIMED MY SWEET SOUL!' Buzzard began running around in little circles while screaming his head off.

All of them would have given anything to make Buzzard stop, except Crush. Crush was in love. This cute little rhino running around the roof of St Paul's had completely stolen his heart and he simply had to cuddle him.

'No don't chase him, Crush,' said Nelson, but it was hopeless. Once Crush fell in love, there was no stopping him.

'Aaaaaaah!' cried Buzzard as Crush chased him, but a sight even more mind-blowing was waiting for Buzzard at the edge of the roof, as he looked out over the city. London looked nothing like the city he had left behind. Compared to his time period, London appeared to have become a sea of lights reaching into the sky. He might as well be on another planet.

'HELL!' he screamed.

'Nope, not hell,' said Nelson, while shooing Crush away from Buzzard. 'I mean, parts of it are bit dodgy, and I s'pose it's changed a lot since your day, but it's not hell,' he went on, pointing up at the dome of the cathedral. 'Look. This bit is still the same.'

'Aaaaaah! Aaaaaah! Aaaaah!' screamed Buzzard, who was now breathing so hard that he passed out and flopped on to his back.

Even though everyone felt Buzzard had every right to freak out, it was a quite a relief to have a bit of quiet for a moment. Crush saw his opportunity, ran to where Buzzard lay and threw his arms around him.

'Well, I don't know about you chaps, but I think he's adorable!' crowed Hoot.

'Is it dead?' said Stan, poking the fluffy ear of the rhino.

'He's not dead. He's alive. In fact, he's very, very much alive.'

Crush's four hands felt Buzzard's belly inflate and

deflate as if it were breathing. The seam that had once only suggested a mouth was now a real fluffy mouth that opened and closed.

'HONK!' said Crush, and Nelson smiled.

'That's right, Crush. We've got Buzzard's soul back,' said Nelson, and he turned to face the others. 'This means we've got bait, and that means the monster is gonna come for it, so we better get to the coast quick as possible.'

Hoot cleared his throat and posed with his wings wide open. 'Well, my dears, I am ready to receive your compliments. Do not hold back. Let your appreciation of me know no bounds, for if I am to make this flight in time, I must be larger and faster than I have ever been before!'

FRINTON-ON-SEA

Though the return of Buzzard's soul had temporarily stopped the monster from wanting to smash things up, it now moved with even more speed and purpose than ever before. The effects of its journey could be seen in the frozen stripe it was leaving behind as it skimmed across the English Channel.

It landed with a tremendous crunch in a potato field and kept rolling until it had smashed a police car parked in a petrol station forecourt. Luckily the policeman was inside the petrol station buying a latte and a Twix at the time. As petrol hissed and sprayed out of the broken

pumps only to freeze in mid-air like giant crystal crowns, the monster sat there panting, its freaky, bloodshot eyes glaring at the world around it. It could tell that Buzzard's soul had moved from its original position. It could even feel the direction it was moving in.

'Buzzard,' it said, and its right wing shot up and pointed in this new direction. It knew Buzzard's position had changed and it was determined to catch up with it as quickly as possible.

Have you ever watched a game show and known the answer to the question only to see the contestant splutter and fail to get it right? 'If that'd been me on there, I would have won first prize!' you exclaim, but the truth is, it is much easier to answer a question when you are sat at home with a nice sandwich and no pressure at all. If it had been you on the game show, it is very likely you would have got it wrong too. All those lights, all those people watching and all those cameras put a great deal of pressure on the brain. The answers may well be in there, but your brain is so squeezed it cannot get at them. I'm only telling you this because it explains why Nelson made the following ridiculous choice.

When deciding which stretch of British coastline would be the best place to battle the monster, Nelson could have selected from any number of appropriate locations. Suffolk and Norfolk alone had plenty of vast beaches and marshlands, all a safe distance from towns and villages. You probably know some great wide-open places too. Though Nelson was not under the glare of TV cameras, he was under a great deal of pressure to save the world, and the only beach Nelson could think of in the heat of the moment was the one he had visited last Easter bank holiday weekend called Clacton-on-Sea.

Rather than an empty field, this was a beach town packed with shops and restaurants and houses and hotels and, to top it all off, a magnificent pier complete with big wheel, roller coaster and novelty attractions. Yep, a stupid place to stage a monster fight.

Realizing his mistake and that things were bound to get messy as they tried to trap a storm-breathing monster and feed it to Nosh, Nelson quickly took his monsters a mile south to Frinton-on-Sea instead, where there was more beach and no pier. Far from ideal, but there was no time to dwell on that now . . .

'See anything?' shouted Nelson over the wind. He meant did anyone see the monster, but the sky was clear but for a few clouds out at sea.

'Nuffin' yet,' said Stan.

All of the monsters were gathered in the sand around Nelson and looking up at the sky, waiting for the monster that was about to be Nosh's dinner.

Nelson pulled the cords on his hood to shut out the wind. Waves of sand snaked their way along the pavement. The windows of the little beachfront hotels were dark, and not a soul could be seen on the street. No cars. No buses or taxis. The emptiness would have creeped out

Nelson had there not been something far creepier on the way. At least the mood was lightened a little by watching Hoot strutting up and down the beach, still at enormous size and singing 'Gangsta's Paradise' by Coolio.

'Let's go over the plan one more time . . . When the monster lands, it'll wanna grab Buzzard straight away, but when I threaten to pull the pin out, the monster's not gonna risk attacking us and losing Buzzard.'

'Unless it's as stupid as Hoot,' Spike added.

'It might be. We don't know. But if it is like Hoot, then it will shrink when you lot start insulting it. And really,

really go for it. Say the worst things you can think of. And when it's small enough, we'll feed it to Nosh, and BOOM! No more monster – right, Nosh?'

Nosh was chewing on a sandal he had found in the sand.

'Don't eat that, Nosh. You're supposed to be working up an appetite,' said Nelson.

'I only chewin' it.' Nosh was drooling so much, it was impossible to look at him and not feel queasy.

'Oh! Mama! Mama! Come quick! What a nightmare I have had!'

It was Buzzard. He was waking up in Crush's arms, his head hidden beneath Nelson's face flannel to avoid him seeing anything that might set him off again. Nelson had hoped Buzzard would have remained unconscious throughout the whole episode, but he was very much awake again.

'Mother! Mother! Come quick! I have dreamed a dream so vivid and vile! 'Twas even worse than the dream in which slugs oozed from my armpits and a donkey would not stop biting my buttocks! Mother! Mother! Bring me frothy milk and gingerbread to settle my nerves!'

'Just be patient with him and leave this to me, OK?' whispered Nelson to his monsters as Buzzard continued to wail. 'He's probably going to freak out again when I take that flannel off his eyes, so why don't you all give us a bit of space.'

All but Crush moved away without dispute. Crush

squeezed Buzzard and honked softly into his rhino ears, but it didn't help at all.

'Mother! Is that you? My dear, you sound like a bugle. A faulty bugle, at that. Hath your nose become blocked with mucus? I suggest we call Doctor Plumley-Pear to smoke out your cloggy nostrils at once.'

Nelson took a deep breath and removed the flannel from Buzzard's eyes.

'Hello again,' said Nelson in his most soothing voice, but it did nothing to stop Buzzard freaking out.

'Oh heavens! Oh no! The giant angel boy! The honking monster! Hell! I am still in hell! And look! My beautiful body remains that of a tiny fluffy thingamajig!'

Crush instinctively hugged Buzzard tighter with all four of his arms while singing, or rather gently honking, a tune into Buzzard's ear. The effect was instant. Like a parent soothing a crying baby with a lullaby, Crush settled Buzzard by gently rocking him in his arms and cooing a simple, soothing melody. Even though he had never heard the tune before, Nelson found himself feeling happier too. When Crush loved someone or something, it really was infectious. Buzzard, the furry little rhino, mumbled something as he snuggled deeper into Crush's chest from which a great wave of love and warmth was radiating.

'Am I a failure? Does everyone hate me?' mumbled Buzzard.

Nelson crouched in front of Crush and spoke to Buzzard

as gently as he could. 'Shh. Shh. Not at all, Mr Buzzard. You're not a failure. In fact, without you, we couldn't save the world. So I suppose that makes you a hero.'

'A hero?'

In that instant, Nelson knew he had just scored a direct hit. Buzzard's vanity was clearly on a par with Hoot's, and appealing to his pride was going to be the key to getting through this without another meltdown.

'Yes. You're a hero. A legend.'

'A legend.' Buzzard clearly liked the sound of that, and Crush pulled him even tighter to his chest.

THE CRASHING CLOUDS

Nelson and Crush had no idea what a huge mistake they had just made.

Not only was Crush filling Buzzard with love and affection, but in trying to appease Buzzard's insecurities, he had flattered his ego, and all of these feelings were being shared with Buzzard's monster. For hundreds of years this wretched creature had been trapped at the bottom of the ocean feeling nothing but anger and pain, and even when it had escaped, it was appalled to find itself as ugly and smelly as a flying cowpat. But everything had suddenly changed. Now the monster could not only feel the irresistible pull of the soul it was born from, but on top of that, new feelings: love and pride. This great dose of warm, sunshiny love and chest-bursting pride made its wings stretch away from its body until they were each the length and breadth of a pirate ship's sails. Every hug and compliment Nelson and Crush dealt Buzzard made his monster's beak – that awful jagged hook jutting out of its face – bubble and crackle as if it were being heated in a furnace, and grow larger and even more threatening. And as the monster's body parts grew, so did the freezing cloud that swirled around it.

There was a tremendous sonic boom. The monster's new bigger and more powerful body had just broken through the sound barrier. Every particle in the air around the creature froze, and the freezing shockwave rippled across the sky over England.

Radars used for tracking aircraft picked up the creature's increased size and monitored its trajectory. The information was relayed to a group of sweaty politicians and generals gathered around a long table beneath a low ceiling in a secret government room. Not one of them had any idea what was flying at the speed of sound over their country, but the decision was instant and unanimous: it was time to engage the military.

As the messages were sent to all British military bases, and the soldiers, pilots and captains were scrambling into action, Celeste Green was dreaming. She should have been home an hour ago, but a flat tyre on her bike meant she had remained at her boyfriend Ivan's house while he mended it for her. Celeste could have easily fixed it herself or just walked home, but Ivan loved any excuse to tinker with a bicycle. His parents had given over the garage at the back of their house to Ivan's passion, and he used the place to mend and even build bikes for people in the neighbourhood. He had fixed the puncture in just a few minutes, but Celeste had already fallen asleep on the big tattered armchair covered in blankets by the log burner. She dreamed of Nelson, leaning out of the window as he had done earlier that day. He leaned too far, and she couldn't stop him falling . . . but he didn't fall. He simply floated upwards. And this was worse. The dream was becoming a nightmare. Nelson was floating further and further away, and there was nothing Celeste could do to get him back.

While she dreamed, Ivan had seized the opportunity to fix two loose spokes, tighten Celeste's terrible brakes, deal with the fifth gear that kept slipping, and adjust her bell so that it rang with a DING! rather than a KLONK!

He was done. The bike was ready. Ivan carried Celeste's helmet and high-visibility jacket over to where she was sleeping. It seemed almost cruel to wake her. She looked so cosy curled up in the chair by the log burner that he considered checking the bike once more to see if there was anything else he could mend.

That's when he felt it.

The vibration of a sonic boom. He had no idea it was created by a monster flying towards his girlfriend's brother.

Celeste's eyes popped open and she gasped.

What was that? she signed.

Ivan shook his head and looked at his workbench, which shook and made the tools upon it dance.

Celeste rubbed her eyes and hauled herself out of the armchair while Ivan pulled on the cord that triggered the garage door to open. The temperature waiting on the other side of the door was colder than a deep freezer. Looking up, she saw something no one on earth had ever seen before.

The few clouds in the sky were slowly crashing into each other.

'Clouds are too soft to crash into each other,' you might say, and if this were a normal night on planet Earth, you would be right. But this was not a normal night. A gigantic monster was flying at twice the speed of sound through the sky over England, freezing the air as it passed, so that what were once fluffy clouds were now mountains of ice falling out of the sky and crashing into each other like badly captained cruise ships.

Celeste grabbed hold of Ivan and pulled him back inside the garage as the first chunk of ice fell. It was the size of a bathtub, and it not only flattened the apple tree in the garden, it rammed the tree several metres below the ground with one almighty smash. Chips of ice flew everywhere like bullets. Celeste leaped up to pull the garage-door cord. The door began to close as the lights went out, and the door stopped moving halfway. Every light in the street went out.

While Celeste tried to pull the door down, Ivan ran to the workbench and ripped back the curtain that hid the logs for the wood burner. With the speed of a squirrel digging to bury its acorn before its friends find out, Ivan cleared the space of logs and turned to Celeste. She was hanging with all her body weight on the garage door to shut it. As it connected with the ground, Ivan reached out his hand, and she ran towards him, both of them ducking under the workbench at the same time. Hailstones performed a never-ending drum roll on the roof.

If another block of ice the size of the last one fell on the garage, it would crush it for sure, but Ivan knew they stood the best chance of survival under the workbench. It had been in this workshop for decades, and though it had taken a billion beatings from tools of every kind, the bench had remained as solid as a rock. Tonight would be the bench's greatest challenge.

Celeste switched on her phone's torchlight and laid it on her lap so that they could see each other.

What's happening? signed Celeste, and Ivan replied, his fingers trembling.

I don't know. We must not go outside. Stay here until it stops.

A great explosion erupted nearby and shook the ground as if to prove him right.

It was the sound of the pub on the corner of their street being crushed by debris from the crashing clouds. Just as the people of France breathed a sigh of relief that the storm cloud responsible for battering their country had gone, the people of England now braced themselves for far worse.

The sky was falling.

THE BATTLE ON THE BEACH

With Buzzard nestled in Crush's arms beneath the face flannel, Nelson stood beside him on the beach, stomping his feet and hugging himself to keep warm. Nosh, Stan, Miser, Puff and Spike were ready to attack and hiding behind the wall that ran the length of the beach.

A lone police car roared by, and Nelson ducked out of sight until its flashing lights had gone. Nelson stood up and felt the temperature suddenly drop even lower. He shivered as the air seemed to tighten around him. From somewhere not too far away came the eerie sound of an air-raid siren. Only very old people who had been alive during the Second World War had heard that sound before, but even those who hadn't been alive at that time felt their skin bristle with goosebumps. It was a sound that everyone on earth instinctively knew meant *run for cover*. Inside their homes, the people of Frinton dashed to their cellars, and if they didn't have a cellar, they dashed under the stairs or the kitchen table or anything they felt might protect them from whatever was about to arrive.

Unlike the people of Frinton, Spike leaped up from behind the wall and began jumping up and down and waving his arms in the air. Nelson had never seen Spike so agile before. He looked like someone following a workout routine.

'Spike? You're supposed to be hiding!'

'It's all right for you, you're not a cactus! I'm ninety-eight per cent water, and if I stop moving, my insides will freeze! I mean, it's hardly the tropical butterfly house, is it?'

Nelson never answered Spike because a screech as loud as a train making an emergency stop on rails made of cats blasted through their eardrums and rattled the brains in their skulls.

The monster had arrived.

Cloaked in its swirling storm cloud, it appeared in the sky above them and dropped on to the beach. BANG!

Sand exploded into the air, and Nelson was knocked off his feet. Winded and temporarily blinded by the sand, Nelson sat up spitting and coughing to find he was looking into the eyes of the monster.

He had never in his life seen anything so ugly.

Seriously, if ugliness were made of rock, then this was Mount Everest.

And on top of its staggering ugliness was the smell. Oh boy, what a stink. A sewer would have seemed like a rose garden compared to the thick rotten stench that filled Nelson's nostrils and made his stomach clench.

The monster tilted its head from side to side while its bloodshot eyes opened wide, looking directly at Nelson's chest where Crush lay holding Buzzard.

Buzzard stirred. 'What on earth is going on? What's that smell? I feel chilly all of a sudden. Would someone please fetch me a scarf? Or another blanket?'

Crush was keeping Buzzard's head buried in his own chest. The monster took a step closer so that its beak was only a metre away from Nelson and Crush. The temperature was so cold now that Nelson felt sleepy. His clothes were solid and cracked like eggshells when he tried to move.

'Come any closer, and I'll release Buzzard's soul! And you don't want that!'

The monster stalled. It said something Nelson couldn't understand and its breath made him gag.

'Quick. Give Buzzard to me, Crush,' whispered Nelson, but Crush didn't want to give up his beloved rhino to this creature.

The monster took another, smaller step closer. It was shaking as if it were nervous or excited. I suppose you would feel excited too if you were about to get something you had wanted for over 350 years.

This time, Nelson didn't even wait for Crush to let go – he just pulled the fluffy rhino out of Crush's arms and held him at arm's length towards the monster, as if Buzzard were a shield. And in an odd sort of way, it was a shield, thanks to Buzzard's reaction to the monster:

'AAAAAAAAAAAAARGH!'

The monster was so surprised to find his master's soul

in the form of a toy rhino that it staggered backwards, its eyes almost popping from their sockets.

'GADZOOKS! WHAT HIDEOUS FREAK OF NATURE IS THIS?!' cried Buzzard, and the monster cowered as if he were a bad dog and Buzzard was his angry master.

Nelson realized this was his moment to make his move and gain the upper hand.

Nelson's own monsters decided to attack right there and then. When I say *attack*, I don't mean they ran at the monster and beat it up; I mean they attacked it with the most painful insults they could all think of.

Oi! Turkey boy!
I'm talking to you, you Kentucky Fried Freak!
You featherless dungheap!
You freaky-beaky berk-a-loid!
You flying haggis!

It was working. The monster was shrinking with every painful insult. On top of that, it was being crushed by the feeling of repulsion and rejection coming from its master, Buzzard.

That's right, you! You great stinking freakazoid!
You look as bad you smell!
Ugly don't even come close to describing what a pile of dog plops you are!
Ya scumbag! Ya snot ball!

Ya disgusting, maggot-ridden, bulgy-eyed, wonky-faced, flabby-gut, twit-brained stink hole!

The monster roared and it twitched as if their curses were knives digging into every part of its body, which grew smaller and smaller until it was no bigger than a very ugly chicken.

Quick as a flash, Stan grabbed the little monster in his huge red hands and lifted it above his head as if it were a trophy.

'GOTCHA!' roared Stan, and the other monsters would have cheered had the smell not gone right up their noses and made them all want to throw up.

'It's worse! The smell o' this thing! Phwooooaar!' Stan held the monster at arm's length and the other monsters roared with disgust, although you could barely hear them over Buzzard, who was still making a heck of a noise.

'Oh shut up, Buzzard. It's your fault this monster exists in the first place,' said Spike, covering his mouth while jumping up and down to avoid freezing.

'What do you mean, *my* fault?'

Before Nelson could stop him from answering, Spike carried on.

'*You* made this monster when *you* lay on that ruddy sin extractor, which is why we needed *you* as bait to catch it.'

'Yeah!' said Stan. 'So now ya both gonna get what you deserve. That's right! We're gonna feed ya both to Nosh!'

'No!' said Nelson, his teeth chattering as he drew breath. 'Just the monster! Leave Buzzard!'

'Suit ya self,' grumbled Stan.

'YEAH! FEED ME DAT LI'L MONSTAH!'

Nosh opened his mouth and drool oozed from the corners. Stan walked towards him with the monster struggling between his fingers while Nosh closed his eyes in order to fully appreciate what he was about to eat.

Stan threw the little monster into Nosh's mouth, which slammed shut like an oven door.

Nelson and his monsters eagerly watched Nosh, waiting for the smoke and flames to erupt from the holes in the top of his head. This was better than TV. Like watching a penalty shoot-out when you knew the striker couldn't fail to score . . .

They waited . . . and waited . . . and Nosh chewed . . . and chewed . . . and then his eyes slowly opened and Nosh began to look uncomfortable.

'What's wrong?' asked Nelson, but Nosh did not reply.

Instead he kept his big mouth shut while his bright pink skin began to turn pale and then a greenish-white. And here it was. The moment that their plan to save the world – which, to be fair, had been going pretty well so far – fell apart.

'Me so sorry, Nelly-son,' groaned Nosh. 'It too disgustin' and ma fire gone out in ma belly.'

'Too disgusting? What are you talking about, Nosh? I've seen you eat much worse than this!'

Nosh's stomach gave an almighty gurgle and he threw up the little monster into the sand. The smell really was spectacularly bad. If you could bottle this scent, it would be called Eau de Death! In fact, it was such an unforgivably bad smell that Nelson was sick.

I know, it's awful to read about someone being sick, but I warned you at the start that things would get nasty. Maybe now is a good time to look at that piglet in pyjamas once again.

'Let me out of here!' cried Buzzard from inside the backpack.

As if this were a call to action, the little monster screamed, sending hailstones like bullets flying in all directions.

As Nelson and his monsters fell to the ground, the monster began to grow once more, the ice and winds swirling around it like a magical cape as it flexed and stretched back into its larger form.

'Well, if it's all right with you chaps, I think it would be better if I stay out of the way for now!' bellowed Hoot, who was still gigantic. And he took to the skies without waiting for a reply.

'NO! HOOT! COME BACK! WE NEED ALL THE HELP WE CAN GET!'

It was too late. Hoot was gone. It was up to the remaining six monsters to do battle.

Nelson grabbed his backpack, swung it over his shoulder and ran back towards the road. The monster lurched towards Nelson, but Stan, Miser and Puff leaped into the storm cloud that now almost entirely hid the monster from view.

There was shouting and howling and a wind so wild and bitter that Spike toppled to the ground like a statue, his entire body frozen so stiff that his outstretched arms snapped off as he fell into the sand.

'Spike!' cried Nelson as he fell on his knees beside him.

From out of the storm cloud swirling around the monster, Stan suddenly appeared – tossed out as if he were nothing more than a rubber ball. His red body slammed into the roof of a frost-covered car parked by the road, making all of the windows explode.

A horrible scream made Nelson turn his head. The monster had Puff clamped in his beak and was shaking him savagely. Gas was leaking out of Puff and mingling with the storm cloud so that it turned purple.

Chomp! Chomp! Chomp!

The monster was chomping down on Puff as if it wanted to bite him in two, but the gas was so powerful and so abundant that the monster began to sway drunkenly. Miser's tentacles were wrapped around the monster's head, which meant he too felt the effects of Puff's gas and fell to the ground.

The monster's eyes rolled back in their sockets and it dropped Puff, broken and limp, into the sand as it collapsed into a deep sleep.

There was pain, cold, misery and disaster whichever way Nelson looked. Nosh was still pale and lying breathless in the sand. Stan had emerged from the smashed car and staggered towards him with one horn missing, cuts all over his skin and one eye swollen shut. A blue lump shifting in the sand near the sea wall suggested Miser was at least able to move. Poor Spike lay frozen and armless in the sand before Nelson, while Puff didn't even appear to be breathing beside the sleeping monster. Where was Hoot . . . ?

Nelson remembered Hoot had taken to the sky and he looked up. There was no sign of him. All Nelson could see were frozen clouds, lit orange by the street lights. And the clouds were doing something he had never seen before: they were crashing into each other just as they had done over Ivan's house. If only Nelson had not been so cold, he would have moved, but all of his joints felt frozen, so he could do nothing but watch as a piece of ice the size of a haystack fell straight towards him from the sky. This was either going to hurt or kill him – either way, there was nothing Nelson could do about it.

Meanwhile, Hoot, who had taken refuge above the freezing clouds, was currently wrapping up a conversation with some passing geese.

'. . . Yes, we were all battling a monster down there. He's the reason for all this cold weather, you know. Now I should probably check on my comrades, but my offer still stands: whenever you're passing London Zoo, do drop in. Lovely to meet you. Safe journey onwards and all that. Toodle-oo!' Hoot flapped his great wings so that he rose a little higher in the sky before diving towards the beach below, where he was about find a very sorry sight indeed.

ARE YOU AWAKE?

It was the middle of the night, but Nelson's parents were wide awake. The sonic boom earlier had woken them, and now they were sat up in bed: Nelson's father on the phone with the doctors tending to Uncle Pogo and Doody, and his mother watching the latest news on television. Celeste had already called them to say she was safe and staying with Ivan just in case any more ice fell, and Nelson had managed to sleep through it all, which made them both very relieved indeed. It was just as well neither parent had bothered to venture further than the doorway of the spare room when checking on Nelson, as they would have clearly seen that what they had thought was the body of their sleeping son was in fact several pillows, and the suggestion of hair merely the back of a Chewbacca mask filled with socks.

The first TV images of ice clouds and the damage they had caused when they fell from the sky were as mesmerizing as they were frightening.

'Look at the state of that pub! It's been squashed flat as a pancake. Lucky no one was hurt. Mind you, I never did like that pub. The bloke that ran it was a right grumpy old fart,' said Tamsin, Nelson's mother, as his father, Stephen, finished his call with the French doctors.

'It's not good,' said Nelson's dad.

'What do you mean, *not good*?'

'Pogo and Doody – they're in a bad way. Really bad. Almost every bone they've got is broken. And also . . . Oh, it's a mess, Tamsin. A horrible mess. The doctors say they might not even make it through the night.'

Nelson's mum put her hand to her open mouth, though she had no words to say, while his dad sat on the edge of the bed, his head hanging over his lap. The thought of losing these two fantastic, larger-than-life men was too awful.

'Hold on, Pogo. Hold on, Doody. Just get through the night, lads,' thought Nelson's dad.

At least he *thought* he'd only said the words in his head, but in fact he had felt them so strongly that he'd said them out loud.

Nelson's mum leaned across the bed and put her arms around him.

'They'll make it through, love. I know they will.'

A hug was just what they both needed. Holding on to each other not only generated warmth but hope.

THE LAND OF EYES

Hoot's jumbo-jet-sized wings beat the salty air, and his great silver beak sliced through the night sky. Nelson and his monsters lay clustered together, protected from supersonic winds deep beneath the feathers on the back of Hoot's neck.

As the saviour of the day, Hoot was now bigger than he had ever been before. He was flying at supersonic speed, singing whatever song he liked louder than a church bell, and loving every minute of it. Nelson's monsters absolutely hated Hoot's singing. He didn't just have a lousy voice; he was now as big as a house, which only magnified how bad it was.

Nelson was waking up and only just realizing where he was. It was a tight fit, but there was comfort in the softness of the giant feathers and the warmth rising from Hoot's body. Nelson had his own additional heat source in the form of Crush, whom Nelson cuddled to his chest; and Crush was comforted in turn by hugging the rhino containing Buzzard's soul and cooing gently into its ear.

'I pulled you out of harm's way in time, Master Nelson,

though you did strike your head on a rock, which accounts for your blackout,' said Hoot.

Nelson rubbed the back of his head. He felt a lump, but only a dull ache to accompany it.

'You were luckier than some of the others,' said Miser, who moved back a little to allow Nelson to see Puff lying next to him.

'Puff? You all right?'

Puff lifted his head from his front paws and revealed a bright blue scar running down the left side of his face. His left eye was closed and swollen. 'Hurts,' said Puff, and he licked his front paws, which were also terribly scarred.

'Puff is not the worst affected, Master Nelson.' Miser was positioned near Nelson's feet and he stretched out a tentacle to lift one of Hoot's feathers.

Beneath the feathers lay Spike. The water inside his

body had expanded as it had frozen so that his green flesh was now swollen and grotesquely deformed, and liquid drizzled out from his needles. The same expression was fixed on his face, but his arms were missing from just below both shoulders.

''Is arms snapped off like twigs in the cold,' said Stan, who was sharing the same feather with Spike.

'They can grow back though? His arms, I mean,' Nelson asked.

Stan shook his head. 'We don't know. Same as my horn. Same as Puff's ear. We might be like this forever.'

Nelson's heart broke and tears came to his eyes.

'Sorry, Nelly-son.'

Nelson looked above to see Nosh still sick and pale, nestled among the feathers closest to the base of Hoot's neck. How could Nelson possibly be angry with Nosh? It wasn't his fault he couldn't stomach the monster.

'Don't be sorry, Nosh. It wasn't your fault. That monster was disgusting . . . Wait, where is it?' Nelson had only just remembered the monster had grown back to full size, and the last thing he remembered seeing was it passing out on the beach from Puff's sleeping gas.

'You will have to crawl carefully to the wing if you wish to see, Master Nelson. But take care not to fall,' warned Hoot. 'Who knows how high we are at this moment . . .'

Nelson placed Crush beside him and crawled across Hoot's shoulders to the base of his left wing. Crawling wasn't easy. The speed they were travelling at forced everything flat so that Nelson didn't so much crawl as *snake* his way to the wing. And this is what he saw . . .

The rope ladder they had 'borrowed' earlier that night from an adventure playground in Regent's Park was now dangling from Hoot's left claw, and the monster was attached to the end of it. It was still very large, and comatose from the overdose of Puff's sleeping gas it had inhaled earlier. Around the monster, a purple storm cloud swirled, leaving a trail of purple ice in the air.

Beneath the monster was blackness. No sign of a road or village to be seen.

'I strapped the monster on, but this was all Miser's idea,' said Stan as Nelson crawled back towards them.

'But why are we carrying it? What are we gonna do with it when it wakes up?'

'Hopefully, it'll be dead before it wakes up.'

'But we can't kill it. You already said – monsters can be injured, but unless you have a fire as hot the sun, they can't be killed.'

'Master Nelson. There is another way,' said Miser.

'What do you mean?'

Miser didn't answer.

'Miser, what do you mean, there's another way? Where are we going?'

'We goin' to da Land of Eyes,' whispered Nosh.

'Land of Eyes?'

'Not the Land of Eyes, ya tiny twit,' snapped Stan. 'It's *Ice* Land. Not Land of Eyes!'

‘Iceland? Why are we going to Iceland?’

‘You cxplain it,’ said Stan to Miser. ‘I was all for telling Nelson from the start, but you lot were too scared about ’im finding out.’

Nelson looked to Miser, who refused to meet his eye as he spoke.

‘At this very moment, we are flying towards Iceland because it is there that we will find an Earth Fire, or as you would call it, a volcano.’ Miser dared to look up and found Nelson staring right at him, desperate for understanding.

‘A volcano is another doorway out of this world for a monster. A doorway that once passed, is closed to us forever.’

‘Why didn’t you tell me before? We could have gone straight to a volcano instead of trying to set Nosh up with a disgusting dinner on a beach!’

‘Forgive us, Master Nelson, but many of us were worried that if you knew how to get rid of us, you would ask us to leave you.’

‘What? Seriously, Miser, why would I do that?!’

‘I knew this was going to happen,’ groaned Puff.

‘You have been most distressed of late, and we feel how much of a burden we have become for you, especially concerning your school life.’

‘No! You’re not a burden, and there is no way I would ever ask you to jump into a volcano.’

‘You have a kind soul and you are our dear friend, but

one day you may feel differently about having monsters in your life, Master Nelson. And when that day comes, and we all know it will, you will want to be rid of us.'

What Miser said rang true for Nelson, but there was no way he was going to accept that truth.

'Rubbish. I will never want you to go.'

'We had hoped, selfishly I know, that if the plan with Nosh had worked tonight, you need never know of this other way.'

If it wasn't for Hoot's singing, this would have been the most miserable Nelson had ever been.

'OK, well . . . So, we're gonna throw this monster into the volcano?'

Miser nodded.

'What if it wakes up before we get there?'

'We're almost there,' wheezed Miser.

'OK. And if we are cut short, we can always toss Buzzard into the volcano, and his monster will have no choice but to follow.'

'NO!' screamed a little voice, and looking down, Nelson saw the fluffy rhino that was Master Buzzard, wriggling in Crush's arms.

'Oh, you could've told me he was awake, Crush!'

'HONK! HONK!'

'No! I will not be used as bait for your devilish schemes! And tossed into a volcano? No! Not I!' cried Buzzard. 'I am a nobleman! I am William Buzzard! And I don't want any part of this! All I want is some cake! Giant boy! Please! I beg of you! Show mercy! Have I not been through enough?'

Time for the hard truth, thought Nelson, but he never had the chance to speak, for at that very moment Hoot let out a terrible cry, and the next thing Nelson knew, he and his monsters were falling through the ice-cold air.

AIR FORCE

The two fighter jets had fired their missiles at the same time.

They had both been aiming for the mysterious purple ice storm cloud that hurtled like a comet at the speed of sound through the night sky, but only one of the missiles had struck the sleeping monster. The other missile had struck Hoot's right wing. Neither pilot could see Hoot or the other monsters or even the twelve-year-old boy falling out of the sky, but they could see the storm cloud falling towards the ocean.

There's nothing like being struck by a missile followed by a dip in the North Atlantic to wake up a dozing monster, and Buzzard's monster woke beneath the waves in a most terrible rage.

'BUZZAAAAAARD!' screamed the monster as it broke the water's surface and flew back into the sky.

The pilots had already begun their return, having watched the storm cloud fall into the ocean below, but once again their radars lit up with the same target as before, this time flying directly towards them.

Both pilots turned their jets around, levelled their

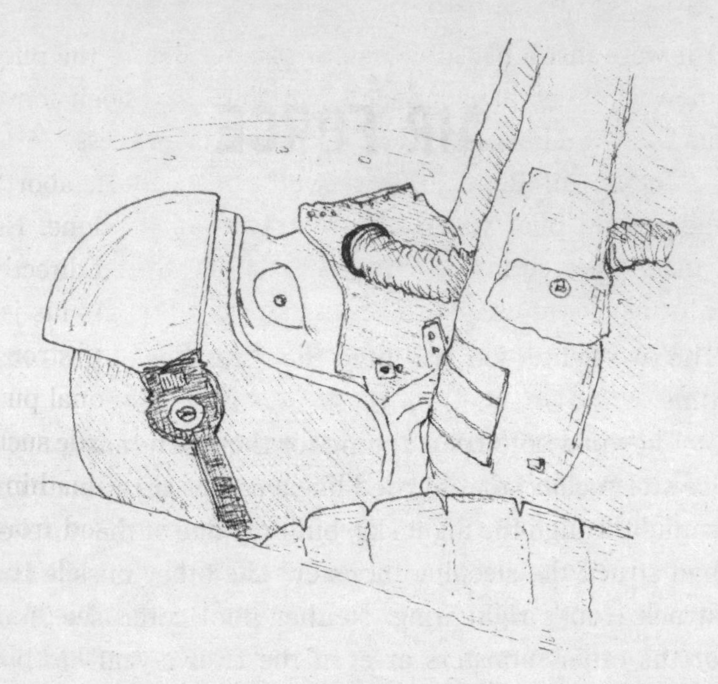

sights with the rising ice cloud and fired their missiles. The monster screeched, and the ice storm that issued from its mouth was so powerful, it froze the missiles solid, and they shattered like glass against its body. The pilots' hail of armour-piercing bullets hit the monster before it had time to take a breath, but no sooner had the wounds appeared than they were gone again. Unlike Nelson's monsters, this one could heal itself instantly. It was indestructible.

The first pilot had no intention of giving up and continued to shoot as he flew straight past the cloud. BOOM! The brave pilot never saw the monster lash out with its wing as he flew by, his jet breaking into pieces as if it were just a big toy made of plastic. Before the pilot knew what had happened, his parachute was open above his head and he was floating in complete darkness.

'Jet down! Repeat! Jet down! Abort, abort, abort!' the second pilot yelled into his radio microphone. He yanked the steering column back and flew the jet directly into the sky to escape the rising storm cloud. As his jet shot towards the stars, the pilot felt two very strong sensations. The first was the powerful gravitational pull that he was used to experiencing whenever he made such a steep ascent. But the second sensation was something he had never felt before. Though he was dressed from head to toe in the warmest of uniforms, he felt the freezing temperature outside creeping through his skin and into his bones. Before he knew it, the entire cockpit, the flight instruments, steering column and even his visor had frozen up. He could feel the powerful vibration of the jet engines stutter and fail, and as he looked out of the left side of his cockpit, he saw the storm cloud rising on a fountain of hail and snow. The pilot's thumb felt around for the eject button, flipped the protective lid and pressed. As his parachute opened, he never saw the giant featherless wing lash out and smash the frozen jet to smithereens.

THE MERCY OF THE SEA

Their mouths were too full of rushing wind to scream, although an awful cry was coming from Hoot. He was spiralling nose-first towards the ground, shrinking and shedding feathers as he fell.

It had all happened so quickly that there was nothing Nelson could to do but claw hopelessly at the rushing wind and wish that he was wearing a parachute instead of a backpack.

A hand was around his throat. It was Stan. His arms were suddenly wrapped around Nelson, squeezing him tightly.

SMASH! was the sound of Stan and Nelson hitting the water, Stan's body taking the full force of the blow. You might think the word 'splash' would be more appropriate to describe the sound of someone falling into the sea, but Nelson and Stan had fallen from a such a great height that it really was more like breaking through a glass wall than hitting water.

Their bodies plummeted through the darkness as quickly as a ship's anchor.

The pressure of the water was tremendous and it

crushed Nelson's ears and chest as if King Kong were using him as a stress reliever. It wasn't just air that was taken out of him. All thought and reason was wiped from his mind as if he were being squeezed out of existence. Nelson did not think of his monsters or of his family or of the fact they had failed to reach the volcano in time. Nelson was unable to think of anything. And even

if he had managed to think to kick out or try and swim upwards, there wasn't enough air in his lungs to bring him back to the surface now. He was at the mercy of the ocean, but lucky for Nelson, the ocean was about to show him a great deal of mercy.

It began with a tugging sensation under Nelson's right arm. The next thing he knew, both shoulders were being pushed upwards, and then the rushing sensation came. He wasn't going down any more. He was going up. Up and up and up. So fast, in fact, that his ears popped. And then SPLASH. Yes, this time 'splash' was just the right word to describe the sound of Nelson's body shooting up and out of the water.

Nelson had no idea what was happening at this point; he only knew that suddenly he could breathe again, and he sucked in great gulping gasps. After he had taken a dozen or so lungfuls of Icelandic sea air and blinked away the salty water, Nelson realized he was once again above the ocean. Only a few metres high this time, but he was not going up or falling into the waves any more. He was being held aloft on a tower of fish.

His brain seized upon the lovely new oxygen that had found its way back into his bloodstream, and Nelson experienced his first real thought since falling into the ocean, and it was this: being admired by fish did have its perks after all.

'Stan!' cried Nelson, but there was no sign of his little red monster.

The tower of fish flapped their tails and squirmed among each other before slowly dropping back towards the water.

'No! Please, I need to get to the land!' cried Nelson.

But he needn't have bothered. The fish knew very well where their human friend needed to go, and it certainly wasn't back into the ocean.

Though his body was now submerged from the waist down, Nelson felt a gentle pressure on the small of his back, and suddenly he was moving forwards. He looked over his shoulder and could see the ripples of fish beneath the surface driving him towards the shore. Nelson shook his head and felt his ears clear of seawater. He flicked his wet fringe out of his eyes. It was still dark. There were no signs of human life, no cities or streets . . . but a distant volcano was painting the clouds red.

THE RACE TO THE VOLCANO

The volcano. The sight of it brought Nelson back to his senses. They were here to throw Buzzard into the volcano so that the monster would follow him to its death. But where was Buzzard now? Where was the monster? And where were his own monsters?

Nelson felt a forceful jolt from behind and he was flung forward on to a narrow rocky ridge. Once he had managed to hold on tight, Nelson turned back to thank the fish, but before he could, he was hit in the face by a very large wave. By the time Nelson had shaken the water and foam out of his ears and eyes, the fish were gone, and another wave was on its way. Nelson braced himself and let the wave smash into him before trying to climb up the rock face.

Reaching up, his fingers scraped around to find another ledge to cling to, but his hands were too numb to feel anything. Another wave flattened him against the rock. Once again he spat out the seawater and reached up, but his numb fingers found nothing but slippery hopelessness. Yet another wave came, crushing him against the rock, and the suck of the undertow almost pulled him back out to sea.

He was frozen to the bone and trapped on a rock being pounded by wave after punishing wave when the biggest wave of all arrived. He couldn't hold on and, once again, he was underwater, only this time he was moving upwards with the wave. When it subsided, Nelson was left lying face down on top of the rock.

'Master Nelson!' came the unmistakeable hissing tones of Miser.

Nelson almost cried out with happiness.

'You're hurt . . . I shall find you something . . .' said Miser, who began to do something Nelson had never seen him do before. Miser took a great deep breath, closed his mouth, held his nose and appeared to sneeze violently without letting any air escape from the usual exits. Now, if you or I did that, we would make our ears pop, but Miser

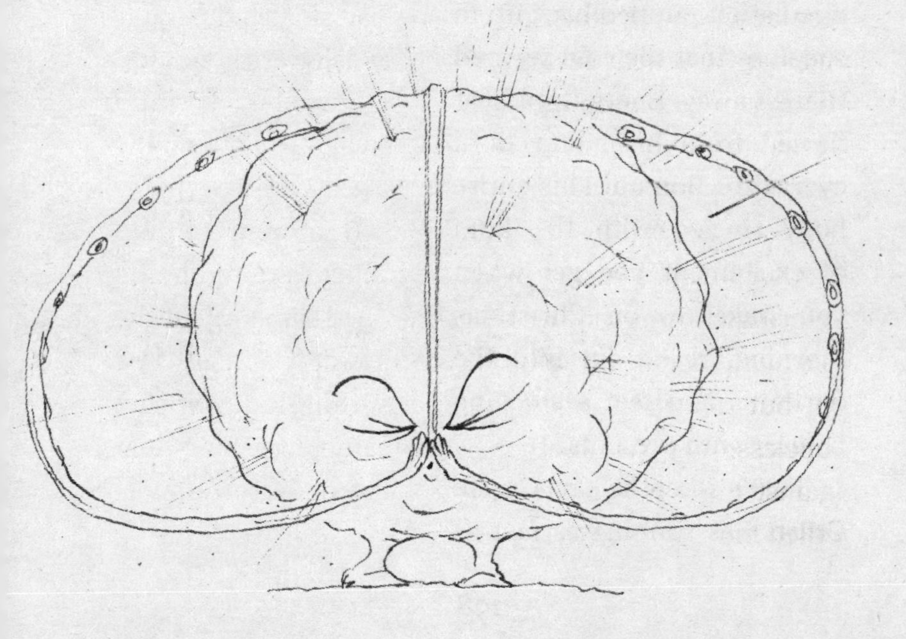

made all of the pockets in his blue body turn inside out.

Everything he had stolen in goodness knows how long came tumbling out of his body. Wallets, phones, cutlery, mirrors, jewellery, money, flashlights, shoelaces, keys and, most importantly of all, a little bottle containing Spike's cactus juice.

'Aha! There it is, Master Nelson! Drink a little and you will be re-energized! Now, I must join the others,' said Miser unscrewing the cap and running out of sight.

Nelson's whole body shook as he put the little bottle to his lips and took a sip.

Once again, the effect of the cactus juice was instantaneous. The achiness in his muscles was kicked out, and his circulation ramped back up to speed so that the cold seemed to melt away. Energy and heat flowed from his stomach in every direction until his entire body tingled with the kind of excitement you get when you wake up on Christmas morning, reach out into the darkness and feel a stocking bulging with presents.

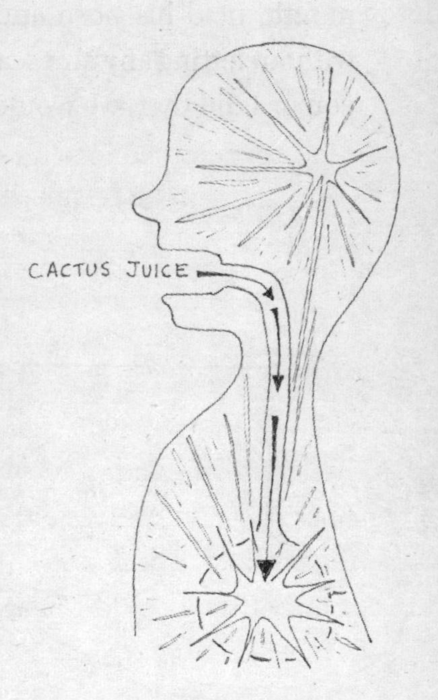

That's when he saw Crush. Crush was running as fast as

he could away from the shore towards the volcano.

'Crush! Wait! Wait for me!' shouted Nelson, but his voice was drowned out by the ear-splitting scream of Buzzard's monster. Nelson turned in time to see it skimming over the ocean and flying towards him.

There was a sound like the crack of a whip, and when Nelson opened his eyes, he saw Miser clinging on to the abomination like a rubbery necklace.

As Miser and the abomination landed, Miser dug his feet into the ground and pulled against Buzzard's monster with all his might. His tentacles stretched until they were almost as thin as kite strings, but Miser did not let go until the abomination turned to spew frost and ice into Miser's face.

Miser was sent flying back towards the ocean, and the monster tumbled forwards.

'RUN, CRUSH!' bellowed Miser, and Crush turned to face him. Even though Crush had gained a great deal of distance, Nelson could now see he was clutching something tightly to his chest with all four arms.

'Curse you, Christopher Wren! 'Tis all your fault that I am in this dire pickle of pickles!' cried Buzzard.

Crush still had hold of the little toy rhino containing Buzzard's soul and was running as fast as he could towards the volcano. There was still a chance the plan could work if only Crush could get there before the monster caught him.

Miser shook off the ice mask the abomination had

given him, and sprang forwards using his ever-so-long arms like a monkey (only with octopus-style tentacles instead of hairy arms).

It was a race to the volcano. A race Nelson's monsters were unlikely to win, for the monster flew at breathtaking speed. Only Hoot could move that quickly, and he had a damaged wing and was nowhere to be seen.

'Typical,' is what Spike would have said had he not been thawing out. His swollen, leaking body lay just a few feet away on the rocks.

'Crush! Look out!' cried Nelson, even though he knew Crush would not be able to hear him.

But Crush did hear him. Not through the air, but through the invisible lines that connected Nelson to all of his monsters, and Crush responded by turning just in time to see the abomination barrelling towards him.

'HOOOONK!'

'TO ME!' came the unmistakeable roar of Stan. He was about one hundred metres to the left of Crush, his eyes glowed red in the dark, and his fists had swollen to twice their normal size. Stan was in his element, even though one of his horns was broken in half.

In that split second before the monster caught up with Crush, Crush gave his beloved little rhino one last big squeeze and threw it to Stan, who jumped, caught it in mid-air, and continued to run towards the volcano. Miser ran straight past Crush, clearly intending to be there to catch Buzzard and carry him further.

In other words, they were playing rugby, only instead of a ball, they were passing a fluffy rhino to each other, and this time the goal wasn't a white line in the grass, but a live volcano. Nelson could only watch as the monsters sprinted into the distance.

But then again, maybe Nelson didn't just have to watch. He could help. All he needed was a bit more of a boost, and just the boost he needed was in the bottle he was holding.

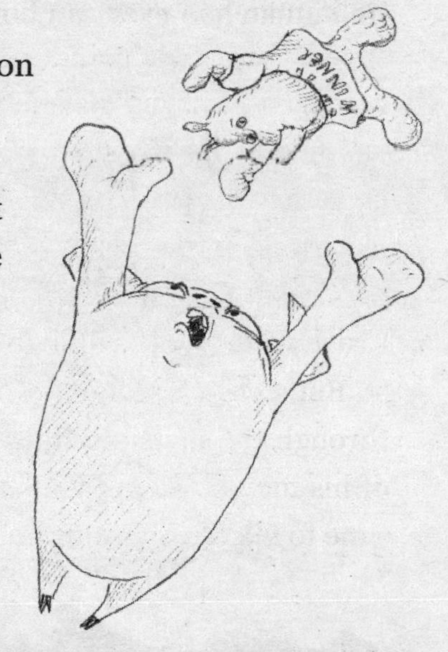

He had never taken more than a sip before, and it had been enough to make him feel fantastic. What would happen if he drank the whole bottle? Would he be stronger or would it make him sick?

Nelson put the bottle to his lips and paused.

Was it dangerous to drink more? Would receiving a large dose of Spike's cactus juice make him pop like a light bulb overloaded with electricity? These are all good and sensible questions to ask in this situation, but Nelson felt that in this case, his own safety was less important than getting that monster into the volcano. So he drank every drop in the bottle.

In the few moments it took for Nelson to push the empty little bottle into the front pocket of his hooded top, his body changed from feeling awful to feeling phenomenal. Warm, strong and lighter than air. He was filled with a thrilling sense of being able to do anything, and just when he thought he could not feel any better, Nelson ran from the spot he'd been standing in at a speed no human had ever run before. His legs were a blur. His

arms pumped faster than the wings of a hummingbird. Nelson was a human rocket on his way to join a game of monster rugby.

'Stan! To me!' cried Nelson, and Stan threw Buzzard just as the abomination pounced on top of him. Nelson jumped and found he was flying through the air in a great arc.

'Waaaaaah!' cried Nelson, but more out of surprise than fear. He caught Buzzard in mid-air, pulled him to his chest and hit the ground, still running.

Up ahead, the volcano sent a jet of orange lava high into the sky. Usually this volcano would just sizzle and smoke quietly for decades on end, but just as the trees and animals of the world had responded to the presence of Buzzard's monster, the volcano had too. It stirred and bubbled and boiled, like a soup awaiting the last, essential ingredient.

'Aaaaargh!' cried Buzzard, pointing a fluffy arm to the sky, and Nelson turned to see the monster sailing through the air towards them with Stan clinging to its back.

Nelson took off again. It felt so good to run this fast, to be a turbo-charged version of himself. And it wasn't just his body that felt this way. He felt he could have played the entire world at chess and win. Every Olympic sport could be his to master, and every record could be smashed. He could have painted a masterpiece, written a song that would remain number one around the world for decades, and maybe taken on brain surgery in his spare time. And while Nelson was thinking these things, his legs were carrying him across black volcanic rock that bled red-hot lava.

The boiling red mouth of the volcano was within reach. Nelson felt its heat like an angry slap to his face. The smoke and ash raced into his lungs. He may have been filled with super-human levels of strength, but Nelson was still made of skin and bone, and if he didn't stop here he would be cooked as quickly as a jacket potato sitting beneath a launching NASA rocket.

It didn't matter that he couldn't get closer. With this new strength, he could easily throw Buzzard in from here.

'Why must I be punished for what I did? Why?! I only wanted to be admired!' wailed Buzzard. 'Is it so wrong to want to be loved and worshipped?'

'Look, I don't know how else to say this, but your stupid vanity literally became a monster.'

Buzzard said nothing. It was, after all, quite a lot to take in.

'Now, Master Nelson! Throw it!'

It was Miser, and he

was doing an excellent job of keeping up with Nelson while Stan continued to wrestle with the abomination, slowing it down. But it was clear that he wouldn't be able to hold it back for long.

'I created this? This abomination was born of my vanity?' Buzzard was appalled.

'Yeah, but you could still be a hero, Master Buzzard. A real hero. You just have to be really brave.'

'The volcano?' said Buzzard.

Nelson looked down at Buzzard, whom he was holding in his right hand, and nodded.

'Now, Master Nelson! Now!' There was panic in Miser's voice for he could see the monster was winning the battle against Nosh and Stan. A few more seconds and it was bound to break free, and Nelson would not be able to outrun it.

The moment had come for Nelson to finish what they had started. To rid the world of Buzzard's monster. All he had to do was throw a toy rhino into a volcano.

'Master Nelson! You must do it now!' Miser was gesturing wildly towards the abomination, who was gaining the upper hand over Stan with terrible blows.

'THROW THAT RHINO INTO THE VOLCANO!' roared Stan.

'I'm sorry, Master Buzzard,' said Nelson.

Though the toy rhino was only made of synthetic fibres, Buzzard's little face appeared to radiate fear. Nelson knew he couldn't dwell on this and drew back his arm, when suddenly everything went black. He was lying face down against the volcanic rock. The monster had broken free and blasted Nelson to the ground with its freezing breath. A layer of clear ice as thick as a duvet covered Nelson from head to toe. His right arm was stretched out to his side, where Buzzard lay.

The monster saw its prize and knew that it had won.

BUZZARD'S CHOICE

Buzzard had fallen free of the ice and was scrambling to his little fluffy feet.

'I know now what I must do,' said Buzzard. 'Goodbye, giant boy, and thank you.' Buzzard began to run towards the volcano.

'BUZZARD!' screamed the monster as it lurched forwards.

Nelson suddenly moved with such tremendous strength that the ice around him exploded in all directions. The monster jerked backwards and turned to find Nelson had hold of its left wing. The cactus juice was still working wonders as it rushed around Nelson's body.

The abomination tugged, but Nelson held on tight, and in return for this, Nelson received another blast of icy wind.

Nelson very quickly crouched down behind the wing, protecting himself as much as he could from the blast.

'RUN, BUZZARD!' cried Nelson.

'I'M RUNNING AS FAST AS I CAN!' cried the little fluffy rhino, whose legs really were a joke. The mouth of the volcano was no more than two hundred metres away, but for legs that small, it might as well have been a mile.

Nelson knew he had only one job to do: hold on.

The monster was not going to play nicely. It slammed its wing down on Nelson as if it were swatting a fly.

I'm fighting a monster with my bare hands! thought Nelson to himself. It was such a spectacular and surprising thing to find himself capable of, that Nelson began to laugh. Every snap of the monster's beak or swipe of its wings only made Nelson laugh more.

From the monster's point of view, this situation was incredibly cruel. For hundreds of years it had yearned for Buzzard, and now it was close enough to touch him, but some annoying and very strong little boy was preventing him from doing so. It was these exact thoughts that drove the monster absolutely bananas.

'BUZZARD!' it screamed, and another thunderbolt struck Nelson. It didn't hurt, but it had a momentary stunning effect, making him lose his grip.

The monster had only just managed to spread its wings when Miser, Stan and Crush leaped on top of it.

The sound they made as they all fought to contain the abomination was truly dreadful, howling and screaming with voices that sounded both angry and in pain. Among the terrible din, a little voice called out.

'I'm so sorry!' cried Buzzard. He was still running as fast as he could towards the mouth of the volcano. His fur was smoking in places, and his little plastic eyes were starting to melt as he drew nearer. Meanwhile the volcano bubbled and burped, sending jets of liquid fire into the sky.

'I may have lived the life of a coward! But I hope that I may die a hero!' Buzzard was almost at the mouth of the volcano. Before him, great towers of steam corkscrewed in the air as they rose from the lava as if to say, 'Come on in! It's warm inside!'

'YOU CAN'T HOLD ON! LET GO!' cried Nelson, and his monsters fell away from the creature. 'JUMP, BUZZARD! JUMP!'

Nelson didn't need to give the command. Buzzard had already decided his fate and he leaped into the steaming hot air. The swirling winds caught him and carried him up and over the mouth of the volcano.

For a moment, Nelson saw the little rhino turn red from the lava below, and then it was gone, followed a split second later by the screaming, hideous monster it had created. The lava swallowed them both up, leaving no trace, not even a bubble on the surface to show that either one had ever existed.

BROKEN MONSTERS

Buzzard was gone. His monster was dead. The world was safe once more. But that did not mean their problems were over. Along with severe bruising and cuts, Stan had lost a horn. Puff was still reeling from the scars he had received earlier, and he had new scars too. Miser had scars to match, though his were purple and covered his face and tentacles, which had been stretched out of shape and lay limp like a skipping rope beside him. It would take a while for these terrible wounds to heal. Crush seemed to be the only one who had escaped injury, although he had begun to cry.

'Crush, it's OK. It's over,' said Nelson. 'I'll get you another rhino, just like that one.'

'Crush ain't cryin' over the toy. 'E's cryin' cos of Spike,' said Stan.

'Where is Spike?' Nelson looked around. Though the light was scarce, Nelson could see the shape of Hoot standing near the ocean beside a lump that he assumed was Spike.

'My flying days are over, chaps,' said Hoot as they all gathered by his side. It really was a sad sight to see him with one wing dragging beside him. 'And I'm not sure dear Spike will ever be the same again.'

Nelson knelt beside their green friend and touched his flesh. It was thawing but it was still so cold, and there was no sign of life.

'He just needs warmth,' said Nelson. 'Let's get him closer to the volcano.'

The monsters carried Spike's body close to a seam in the rock where lava slowly oozed like honey. The heat was tremendous, and they all backed away, shielding their faces.

The first change they saw was in Spike's eyes, which had been bulging terribly. He blinked, and Nelson and his monsters cheered. Then Spike's mouth flexed a little as if trying to speak, but before he could say a word, a great hissing sound came from inside his body, and green juice began to spray from all the tiny needles in his skin.

'Ha ha! He's coming back to life!' Nelson said, laughing as juice sprayed everywhere.

'Water bottle!' said Nelson, thinking out loud, and dug the little bottle out of the pocket of his hooded sweater.

Spike's body had already lost its swollen shape and, more importantly, his shoulders had begun to sprout new arms.

'Oooow!' moaned Spike as Nelson filled the bottle with the liquid spraying out of his needles.

'Good idea, Master Nelson,' said Miser as he flexed his

beautifully restored tentacles. 'Save some juice for future emergencies.'

Nelson stood up and looked around. The volcano had begun to return to its quiet smoking state, and the sky was dark but for the stars. Nelson had never felt so completely alive in his life.

'Oh man,' said Nelson turning quickly to face his monsters. 'I still feel amazing. That juice, it's made me feel like I could lift up a house or . . .' He tailed off and looked at his watch.

'Three hours and seventeen minutes,' he said, and stuffed the bottle into his backpack before swinging it on to his shoulder.

'Master Nelson,' said Miser, sounding concerned. 'You're not thinking of going through with the school exam?'

'Yep. I've never felt more clever in my life! But first, we have to visit my uncle Pogo and his friend Doody. Hoot! We have three hours and seventeen minutes to get to France and then back to my school. And if anyone can do it, you can, you fabulous, fantastic and wonderful bird!'

'Dear boy!' exclaimed Hoot, whose head had already begun to swell in size. 'I shall be only too happy to oblige!'

HOSPITAL FOOD

One hour and eight minutes later, Spike, Hoot, Stan, Puff and Miser waited patiently on the roof of the French Hospital, while Nelson, Nosh and Crush were sneaking into the room in which Uncle Pogo and Professor Doody were being treated.

None of the security cameras ever caught a glimpse of Nelson as he was hiding inside Nosh. Those of you familiar with Nelson's story will know that although Nosh has a huge belly in which Nelson can hide from human sight, as a hiding place it is both disgusting *and* has a very strict time limit. Unless you happen to be a disgusting monster, Nosh's belly cooks whatever he eats, and so Nelson had to be out of there before being roasted alive.

Crush was rolling Nosh down the hospital corridors like you would roll snow to build a snowman. Twice he almost ran into a member of staff before rolling Nosh through the doors of Doody and Pogo's room.

'Bleaurgh!' said Nelson as he fell out of Nosh's mouth covered in slobber.

'You OK, Nelly-son?' whispered Nosh.

'You don't need to whisper, Nosh. No one else can hear you.'

Nelson got up from the floor clutching his water bottle and turned to face his uncle Pogo and Doody.

He was shocked at what he saw and felt tears spring to his eyes.

Both men were asleep, with tubes coming out of their arms. Their limbs were encased in plaster, and through the plaster, metal rods protruded.

They were broken like toys, and all because he had chosen to do nothing.

Well, at least he could do something now.

Nelson could hear people moving and talking in the corridor. He had to move fast.

Unscrewing the cap of the bottle, he held it to his uncle's lips and poured the cactus juice into his mouth.

By the time Nelson and his monsters were halfway back to London, Doody and Pogo were wide awake, their bones healing at a miraculous speed. The only negative side effect was that the two of them were straight back to telling their usual awful jokes.

WHERE IS NELSON?

While everyone else in France and England rejoiced that the strange ice cloud had disappeared once and for all, Nelson's family was completely on edge as they waited for Mrs Vigars, the head teacher of Nelson's school, to answer the phone.

'Good morning, Mrs Green,' said Mrs Vigars. 'How can I help you?'

'Well, I'm sorry. I don't know what's happened to him. Nelson, I mean. I thought he was still in bed, but I just went to check, and he's not there, and I don't think he's even slept in his bed and there's no sign of—'

'He's here,' interrupted Mrs Vigars.

'He's what?'

'The test. He's sitting it right now. It started just a few minutes ago.'

Nelson's mum was so relieved that she completely forgot to ask any questions about how and when Nelson got to school. She sank on to the bottom step of the stairs and shook her head. Celeste and Nelson's father breathed a huge sigh of relief.

'Of course, we weren't expecting any students in school

today after what happened with the storm last night, but your son insisted on taking the exam as planned, so . . . well, he's sitting it right now,' said Mrs Vigars before chuckling and popping a chocolate mini egg into her mouth.

Nelson had just reached the last question on his exam paper, but he already knew he had passed, and knowing this made him smile and bounce his knee up and down. He really, really, really needed to pass this test and prove to his school and his parents that he was, to use their phrase, turning a corner. But just as he began to write his final answer, Nelson's eyelids began to feel heavy. He shook his head and tried again to write, but his vision began to blur.

The teacher on duty for Nelson's exam was too interested in reading the latest news on his phone about the 'rogue storm' and the giant mountains of ice to notice his solitary student not only falling asleep, but sliding off his chair and on to the floor.

'Oh, you've gotta be jokin',' said Stan with a groan.

He, along with Nosh, Hoot, Crush and Miser were watching Nelson through the classroom window. Nelson had forbidden them from being in the same room as him (last time it had ended in the school hall burning down!), but even if they had ignored his demands, there was nothing they could do to help him now. The effects of the cactus juice had worn off, and Nelson had fallen into a sleep that would last a little over twenty-four hours.

YOUR GOOD HEALTH

That week, along with a massive clear-up campaign, there were parties all over France and England to celebrate the disappearance of the ice storm, but the best party of all was held in Nelson's kitchen. They were celebrating the extra good news of Uncle Pogo and Doody's miraculous recovery *and*, on top of that, Nelson's success in his exam. Despite having missed thc last question and fallen asleep at his desk, Nelson had passed with flying colours. All that remained for Nelson to do was to compete in the final rugby match, which he was actually looking forward to this time.

'Your good health!' said Nelson's dad, raising a glass to Doody and Pogo.

'Good health?' said Doody. 'Mate, I've never been in better shape me whole life!'

'Me too,' said Pogo. 'Those French doctors worked some kind of magic on us.'

'Shame they couldn't do nothin' about that ugly mug o' yours though,' said Doody, which made everyone laugh.

'Nelson Green! Don't just scoop the peas into your mouth off the plate! You look like a dustpan and brush!

Use a knife and fork like a normal person,' said Nelson's mum before finishing her white wine and holding the empty glass out towards Nelson's father for a refill.

Nelson laughed, and Celeste laughed too. She signed to Ivan, who then laughed louder than all of them. It was the first time Ivan had joined them for dinner, and he had contributed by making shortbread for dessert. Nelson could not wait to eat it.

'Why have you got paint on your hands?' asked Nelson's mum, and Celeste caught his eye. There were green, yellow, red and blue splodges of paint on both sides of his hands, but he was not going to tell his mother the truth as to how they got there, and so he lied. Just a little bit.

'I was painting . . . some stuff,' he said.

'Well go and wash them right now!'

Nelson pumped liquid soap into his hands and rubbed them together until there were bubbles galore.

'Pssst!' said Stan who was peering in through the toilet window.

'What's wrong?' said Nelson.

'We're ready when you are.'

'OK. Well, we're going to finish dinner first, and then I need you to take Puff around the houses to sort out the neighbours. He can do my mum and dad last.'

'Got it.' Stan let go of the window ledge and there was a crunch as he landed in a pile of leaves below.

Nelson rinsed his hands and smiled as he dried them on the towel. Tonight was going very well indeed, and there was freshly baked shortbread waiting for him downstairs.

NICE TO MEET YOU

It was way past midnight. Nelson's mum and dad were fast asleep. The television at the end of their bed was still on, but there was no chance of them waking up because their room was filled with Puff's purple gas.

Outside in the garden, Celeste and Ivan sat cross-legged on the grass with their eyes closed.

'Are you sure Mum and Dad won't wake up?' said Celeste.

'Yep. They won't be awake until the morning,' Nelson replied from behind the shed. 'Now, keep your eyes closed.'

'They are closed.' She lay back on the grass, and Ivan lay down next to her. The air was warm and smelt of jasmine, cut grass and the creosote of a freshly painted fence. Ice still hung around in the kerbs and gutters of their street, so there was always the sound of a trickling stream.

Nelson peeped around the side of the shed. Was he right to do this? Was he about to ruin everything by revealing his secret to his sister and her boyfriend? It had seemed like such a good idea on the way home from

Iceland. The cure to all the anguish and confusion he had been weighed down by for so long simply lay in sharing his secret. And in a way that his sister would believe this time.

'Get on with it,' said Stan.

'OK, but one at a time. I'll call you when I'm ready.'

Nelson knelt in the grass in front of his sister and Ivan, who were still lying down. The shed was behind Nelson, and behind the shed were his monsters, nervous as if about to perform on a stage.

'I'm going to introduce you to each one, OK? Now, they're normally invisible, so I've had to decorate them so you can see them.'

While Nelson was saying this, Celeste was translating his words into sign language for Ivan.

'And you won't be able to hear them, only I can, but I can tell you what they're saying.'

Celeste finished signing to Ivan and sat up on her elbows. 'Can they hear us?' she said, and then she gasped. Her shoulders rigid. Her eyes wide.

Ivan sat up quickly and followed her gaze.

Looking past Nelson, they both saw something looking back at them.

Nelson turned. 'Nosh! You were supposed to wait until I called you out. Urgh! Well, you might as well come out now.'

Nelson turned back to face his sister and Ivan, who were dumbstruck.

‘This is Nosh. He’s the greedy one. In real life he’s like a big pink blob, but I’ve painted around his eyes and mouth and put some gloves and socks on him so you can get an idea of his shape.’

To Celeste and Ivan, it looked as if a child’s painting of a face were floating towards them. Nelson had traced Nosh’s features with paint like a clown would use make-up. He was even wearing a small party hat.

‘Nosh says, “Hello.”’

Celeste was vibrating with shock. Her mind was racing so fast, it was in danger of flipping out. Ivan took her hand and squeezed it. She looked at him, and he smiled and laughed as if this was the greatest thing he had ever seen. Nelson’s instinct to bring Ivan along had paid off. He didn’t know why, but Nelson had felt sure Ivan would help Celeste process what he was going to show her.

‘Is that his mouth?’ she said, though in barely a whisper.

‘Yes. His mouth is massive, and he eats all the time. Look, I’ll get him to show you.’

Nelson got up and grabbed a log from the pile beside the back door. He passed it to Nosh, who chomped it down like a turbo-charged electric pencil sharpener.

Ivan laughed out loud and clapped with joy, which in turn made Celeste laugh too.

Nosh looked very pleased with himself as flames roared from the top of his head, but no one was as happy or as relieved as Nelson.

What a sight they all were. Seven monsters sat in a circle, their faces painted and their bodies dressed in all sorts of ridiculous things in order that Celeste and Ivan could see them. You can't blame them for looking silly. They were monsters, not fashion designers. Stan's horns had been taped in tennis racquet grip strip, with tennis balls stuck to their ends to avoid any accidents. A pair of red braces stretched over his shoulders held up a pair of red swimming shorts, while on his hands Stan wore an old pair of oven gloves.

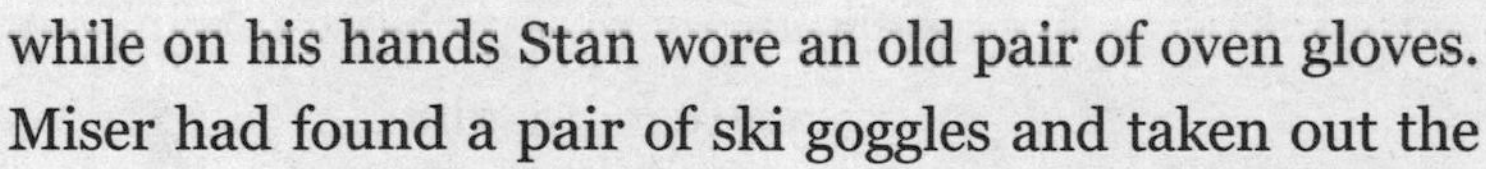

Miser had found a pair of ski goggles and taken out the lenses, which made him look like a racing driver. He had also wrapped fairy lights around his long arms, and they were powered by a battery pack tucked into one of his pockets. Hoot had donned a

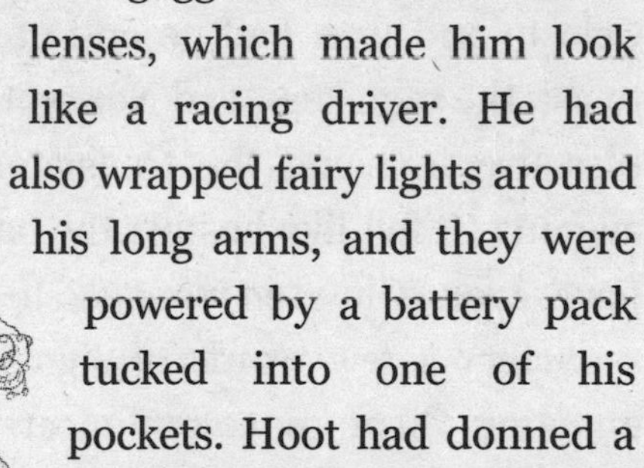

yellow poncho that no one in Nelson's family wore any more and completed his look with a top hat and walking stick that he had painted gold himself. Crush wore the Babygro that Nelson had worn as a newborn baby (and his mother had refused to give away). Crush's great hooter mouth was painted red, and there were bright blue circles around his eyes. Puff had simply covered himself from head to toe in tinsel and glitter, while Spike had made an extra-special effort for this momentous occasion. As clothes of any kind would only snag on his cactus needles, Spike had spent the day sticking Nelson's mother's pastel-coloured cotton balls on to their ends.

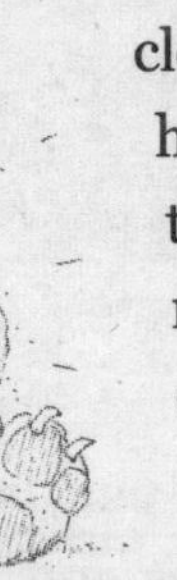

As you can imagine, Celeste and Ivan had no end of questions to ask the monsters, and Nelson took great pleasure in being the translator for the evening. It felt like hosting the best dinner party ever. Ivan even managed to teach the monsters a few words of sign language, enabling them to communicate directly with him. Though they talked long and loud into the night and ate a great deal of Fruit & Nut chocolate, there was no chance of their neighbours spotting what was going on. Every house within earshot had been visited earlier by Puff, and he had left them all filled with enough purple gas to last until morning.

Celeste yawned and rubbed her eyes. They had been out here for hours, and their legs were numb from sitting on the ground.

'We should probably go to bed now,' said Nelson, and the monsters groaned. 'They're groaning. They don't want to go either.'

'All right,' said Celeste.

Ivan tapped Celeste's shoulder and signed to her.

'Ivan wants to know where they will all go tonight.'

'Well, they'll get cleaned up and then head back to the zoo. They can't stay here. Like I said before, they get in too much trouble.'

Celeste relayed this to Ivan, who signed back.

'Ivan has his own workshop at the back of his parents' house. His parents are deaf too, so as long as your monsters stay out of sight, it's safe for them to stay there for now, if they want.'

Nelson's monsters did not need any persuading. Though they would miss their friends at the zoo, being closer to Nelson was everything they wanted. They cheered and jumped and punched the air in triumph before surrounding Celeste and Ivan in a group hug.

Nelson grinned. 'I think that's a yes,' he said as he stood up and watched his monsters waddle after Ivan.

Celeste put her arm around Nelson's shoulders. 'And you definitely need some sleep. You've got that rugby match tomorrow.'

'Will you come and watch?'

'Course. Do you think your monsters will come too?'

Nelson smiled.

He knew they wouldn't miss it for the world.